進階英文 下

鄧慧君　編著

三民書局

網路書店位址　http://www.sanmir.com.tw

© 　進階英文下

編著者　鄧慧君
發行人　劉振強
著作財
產權人　三民書局股份有限公司
　　　　臺北市復興北路三八六號
發行所　三民書局股份有限公司
　　　　地址／臺北市復興北路三八六號
　　　　電話／二五○○六六○○
　　　　郵撥／○○○九九九八──五號
印刷所　三民書局股份有限公司
門市部　復北店／臺北市復興北路三八六號
　　　　重南店／臺北市重慶南路一段六十一號
初版一刷　中華民國九十年二月
編　　號　S 80359
行政院新聞局登記證局版臺業字第○二○○號

ISBN　957-14-3240-7　（平裝）

前　言

　　本書係針對具有基礎英文能力之學生所設計的教材，目標在提供進階英文能力之訓練，及科技人文相關內容知識之吸取。

　　選文方面以「生活化、趣味化、多元化」為原則，配合每課之主題，均有一篇課文及一篇課外閱讀。每課包含詞類變化 (Word Forms) 及句型練習 (Sentence Patterns) 兩部份，配合課文中出現的例字、例句，讓學生從語境中作即時的練習，以增強學習效果。其次，習題 (Exercise) 中的 Discussion Topics 部份，提供教師與課文內容相關的一些課題，使學生能將本身的經驗與課文連接在一起，作為課堂討論或寫作練習之參考。此外，每課的課外閱讀 (Outside Reading) 部份，由教師依上課時間之多寡，可於課堂中講授，或指定學生自行研讀，並可藉由 Reading Comprehension，檢視學生理解的程度。最後，每課後面附有英語學習策略 (English Learning Strategy)，透過淺顯易懂的圖文介紹，使學生的英文學習達到「事半功倍」的最佳效果。

　　本書雖精心編纂，但仍難免有疏漏之處，尚請方家讀者，不吝指正。

鄧慧君　謹誌

2000 年 5 月

略語表

Adj.	形容詞
Adv.	副詞
Aux.	助動詞
[C]	可數
Conj.	連接詞
Int.	感嘆詞
N.	名詞
N.P.	名詞片語
O.	受詞
O.C.	受詞補語
P.P.	過去分詞
Prep.	介系詞
Pron.	代名詞
S.	主詞
S.C.	主詞補語
[U]	不可數
V.	（原形）動詞
Vi.	不及物動詞
V-ing	現在分詞、動名詞
V.P.	動詞片語
Vt.	及物動詞

Contents

Acknowledgements

Texts

◎The Statue of Liberty

From ALL ABOUT THE USA, A CULTURAL READER by Milada Broukal & Peter Murphy. Copyright (c) 1991. Reprinted by permission of Addison Wesley Longman, Inc.

◎Yellowstone National Park

From INTRODUCING THE USA, A CULTURAL READER by Milada Broukal & Peter Murphy. Copyright (c) 1993. Reprinted by permission of Addison Wesley Longman, Inc.

◎Job Interview

From COMMUNICATOR II by Molinsky/Bliss, (c) 1995. Reprinted by permission of Prentice-Hall, Inc., Upper Saddle River, NJ.

◎Quiz: What Kind of Job Is Best for You?

From SPECTRUM 4 by Warshawsky/Byrd, (c) 1994. Reprinted by permission of Prentice-Hall, Inc., Upper Saddle River, NJ.

◎Eskimo Art

From INSIGHTS AND IDEAS, A BEGINNING READER FOR STUDENTS OF ENGLISH AS A SECOND LANGUAGE, Second Edition by Patricia Ackert and Anne L. Nebel. Copyright (c) 1996 by Harcourt Brace & Company, reprinted by permission of the publisher.

◎Body Painting

From BODY LANGUAGE-CODES AND CIPHERS-COMMUNICATING BY SIGNS, WRITING AND NUMBERS. Published by Wayland (Publishers) Ltd. Reprinted by permission of the publisher.

◎Breakfast

From SEEING MORE OF THE WORLD by Alan Turney and Yasuo Kawabei. (c) 1990 Seibido Publishing Co., Ltd., Japan. Reprinted by permission of the publisher.

◎The Right Spot

From PROJECT ACHIEVEMENT: READING B. Copyright (c) 1982 by Scholastic Inc. Reprinted by permission of Scholastic Inc.

◎How Much Exercise Do We Really Need?

From SPECTRUM 3 by Byrd, (c) 1994. Reprinted by permission of Prentice-Hall, Inc., Upper Saddle River, NJ.

◎Health Tips for Travelers

From READING POWER, Second Edition, by Beatrice S. Mikulecky/Linda Jeffries. Copyright (c) 1998. Reprinted by permission of Addison Wesley Longman, Inc.

◎When in Japan

From SPECTRUM 2 by Costinett/Byrd, (c) 1994. Reprinted by permission of Prentice-Hall, Inc., Upper Saddle River, NJ.

◎The Eco-tourist

From MOVE UP by Simon Greenall, published by Heinemann Publishers (Oxford) Ltd. (c) 1995. Reprinted by permission of Heinemann Educational Publishers, a division of Reed Educational & Professional Publishing Ltd.

◎You Love Animals, but Do You Know...?

From CHARLIE BROWN'S SUPER BOOK OF QUESTIONS AND ANSWERS. (c) 1976. Reprinted by permission of United Feature Syndicate, Inc.

◎Animal Communication

From BODY LANGUAGE-CODES AND CIPHERS-COMMUNICATING BY SIGNS, WRITING AND NUMBERS. Published by Wayland (Publishers) Ltd. Reprinted by permission of the publisher.

◎UFOs: Fact or Fiction?

From SPECTRUM 4 by Warshawsky/Byrd, (c) 1994. Reprinted by permission of Prentice-Hall, Inc., Upper Saddle River, NJ.

◎Lost in the Bermuda Triangle

From PROJECT ACHIEVEMENT: READING A. Copyright (c) 1982 by Scholastic Inc. Reprinted by permission of Scholastic Inc.

Unit 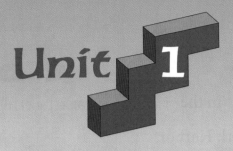 1

The Statue of Liberty

What do you see in the picture?

What does the statue have in its hand?

Have you ever visited the Statue of Liberty?

One of the most famous statues[1] in the
world stands on an island in New York Harbor.
This statue is, *of course*, the Statue of Liberty.
The Statue of Liberty is a woman who holds a

5   torch[2] up high. Visitors can go inside the statue.
The statue is so large that as many as twelve
people can stand inside the torch. Many more
people can stand in other parts of the statue. The
statue weighs[3] 225 tons and is 301 feet tall.

10   The Statue of Liberty was *put up* in 1886. It
was a gift to the United States from the people of
France. Over the years France and the United
States had a special relationship.[4] In 1776 France
helped the American colonies[5] gain[6] independ-

15   ence[7] from England. The French wanted to do
something special for the U.S. centennial,[8] its
100th birthday.

      Laboulaye was a well-known[9] Frenchman
who admired[10] the United States. One night at a

20   dinner in his house, Laboulaye *talked about* the
idea of a gift. Among Laboulaye's guests was the
French sculptor[11] Frédéric Auguste Bartholdi.

statue [ˈstætʃu]

torch [tɔrtʃ]

weigh [we]

relationship
  [rɪˈleʃənˌʃɪp]
colony [ˈkɑlənɪ]
gain [gen]
independence
  [ˌɪndɪˈpɛndəns]
centennial [sɛnˈtɛnɪəl]
well-known [ˈwɛlˈnon]
admire [ədˈmaɪr]

sculptor [ˈskʌlptɚ]

Bartholdi *thought of* a statue of liberty. He offered to design the statue.

Many people contributed[12] in some way. The French people gave money for the statue. Americans designed and built the pedestal[13] for the statue to stand on. The American people raised[14] money to *pay for* the pedestal. The French engineer Alexander Eiffel, who *was famous for* his Eiffel Tower in Paris, *figured out* how to make the heavy statue stand.

In the years after the statue was put up, many immigrants[15] came to the United States through New York. As they entered New York Harbor, they saw the Statue of Liberty *holding up* her torch. She symbolized[16] a welcome[17] to a land of freedom.[18]

25
30
35

contribute

[kən'trɪbjʊt]

pedestal ['pɛdɪstl̩]

raise [rez]

immigrant ['ɪməgrənt]

symbolize ['sɪmbl̩ˌaɪz]

welcome ['wɛlkəm]

freedom ['fridəm]

A. Vocabulary

1. **statue** [ˈstætʃu] *n.* [C] a large sculpture of a person or an animal, made of stone, marble or some other hard material 雕像；鑄像

   Patricia bought a large *statue* of Venus and put it in the living room.

2. **torch** [tɔrtʃ] *n.* [C] a long stick with burning material at one end 火炬

   They hand on the *torch* to the next generation.

3. **weigh** [we] *vi.* to be heavy 重有（若干）

   How much do you *weigh*? I weigh 100 pounds.

4. **relationship** [rɪˈleʃənˌʃɪp] *n.* [C] a connection or association 關係

   The U.S. has good *relationships* with many countries.

5. **colony** [ˈkɑlənɪ] *n.* [C] a country controlled by a more powerful country 殖民地

   India used to be England's *colony*.

6. **gain** [gen] *vt.* to obtain or win 獲得；得到

   He *gained* the first prize.

7. **independence** [ˌɪndɪˈpɛndəns] *n.* [U] the state that a country has its own government and is not ruled by any other country 獨立；自主

   In 1816, Argentina declared its *independence* from Spain.

8. **centennial** [sɛnˈtɛnɪəl] *n.* [C] a centenary; one hundredth year anniversary 一百週年紀念

   This primary school held a *centennial* ceremony last Sunday.

9. **well-known** [ˈwɛlˈnon] *adj.* famous or familiar by a lot of people 眾所周知的

   Arnold is a *well-known* actor.

10. **admire** [ədˈmaɪr] *vt.* to like and respect very much 讚賞；欽佩

    I *admire* the speaker's speech.

11. **sculptor** [ˈskʌlptɚ] *n.* [C] someone who creates sculptures　雕刻家

　　Do you know who is the *sculptor* of the Statue of Liberty?

12. **contribute** [kənˈtrɪbjʊt] *vi.* to say or do things to help to make things successful
　　貢獻；促成

　　Her efforts *contributed* to the project a lot.

13. **pedestal** [ˈpɛdɪst!] *n.* [C] the base on which something such as a statue stands
　　基座；根基

　　The sculpture was built on a bronze *pedestal*.

14. **raise** [rez] *vt.* to collect or bring together (money)　籌募

　　They are *raising* funds for the expedition.

15. **immigrant** [ˈɪməgrənt] *n.* [C] a person who has come to live in a country from
　　some other country　移民

　　There used to be two illegal *immigrants* living next to my house.

16. **symbolize** [ˈsɪmbl̩ˌaɪz] *vt.* to be used or regarded as a symbol
　　of something　做為⋯的象徵；象徵

　　A lily *symbolizes* purity.

17. **welcome** [ˈwɛlkəm] *n.* [C] the act of greeting or receiving
　　gladly　歡迎

　　I gave Tom a warm *welcome* when he visited me last week.

18. **freedom** [ˈfridəm] *n.* [U] the right to do anything you want　自由；自主
　　Today we have the *freedom* to decide our own futures.

B. Idioms & Phrases

1. **of course** suggesting something is normal, obvious, or well-known　當然
　　He has, *of course*, read my application form before the interview.

2. **put up** to construct　蓋；建立
　　John *put up* a new fence at his home.

3. **talk about** to discuss 談論

Those girls are *talking about* the popular Japanese soap opera.

4. **think of** to consider 想到

You never *think of* anyone but yourself.

5. **pay for** to provide the money for something 支付

Students have to *pay for* the textbooks.

6. **be famous for** to be well-known for something 以⋯聞名

New Orleans *is famous for* its cuisine.

7. **figure out** to succeed in solving or understanding something 想出

It took me one hour to *figure out* how to start the machine.

8. **hold up** to have something in hand and move it upwards 舉起

My father used to *hold* me *up* to watch the performance on the stage.

C. Word Forms

1. **v. + -or → n.**

visit（參觀） → visitor（參觀者）
sculpt（雕刻） → sculptor（雕刻者）

EX Jenny is learning how to **negotiate** with people.

She wants to be a good **negotiator** in the future.

2. **n. + -ize → v.**

symbol（象徵）→ symbolize（做為…的象徵）

real（現實） → realize（實現）

special（特別）→ specialize（使特殊化）

 He was sent to the **hospital** yesterday.

He was **hospitalized** by cancer.

 牛刀小試

1. The _____ (sense) can receive signals when the door is opened.

2. She is an _____ (operate) in that trading company.

3. The factory plans to _____ (standard) the production line.

Evergreen Trading Co.

D. Sentence Patterns

1. **S. + help + O. + (to) 原形 V.（幫忙；協助）**

 In 1776 France **helped** the American colonies **gain** independence from England.

(1) Yesterday I **helped** James (to) **write** an English letter.

(2) Please **help** me (to) **move** this table to the corner.

2. $$S_1 + VP_1 + so + \begin{cases} Adj. \\ Adv. \end{cases} + that + S_2 + VP_2 \text{（如此…以至於）}$$

 The statue is *so* large ***that*** as many as twelve people can stand inside the torch.

(1) Eric studied *so* hard ***that*** he passed the test.

(2) Alan was *so* nervous ***that*** he could hardly talk.

 牛刀小試

1. I _____ my mother clean the living room because she was sick.

2. Tom was so lazy _____ his boss fired him.

   (a) as   (b) that   (c) but   (d) than

3. 潔西卡是如此的聰明，以至於所有的老師都喜歡她。

   Jessica is _____ intelligent _____ all teachers like her.

E. Exercise

I. True/False: *Decide true (T) or false (F) of the following statements based on the text.*

❶ The Statue of Liberty is a man who holds a torch up high.

❷ As many as twelve people can stand inside the torch.

❸ In 1776 the American colonies gained independence from France.

❹ It was Laboulaye that designed the Statue of Liberty.

❺ The Americans raised money to pay for the pedestal of the statue.

II. Vocabulary Review: *Complete the sentences with the following words of appropriate forms.*

gift	relationship	gain	design	independence
heavy	contribute	immigrant	visitor	symbolize

❶ He _____ the first prize by hard working.

❷ Cathy hopes to receive a _____ from her parents on her birthday.

❸ Several illegal _____ were found in that factory this morning.

❹ The other day we had some _____ from Switzerland.

❺ In 1816, Argentina declared its _____ from Spain.

❻ Bill _____ to the fund.

❼ This beautiful garden was _____ by my father two years ago.

❽ This luggage is too _____ for me to lift.

❾ The fall of the Berlin Wall _____ the end of the Cold War between East and West Germany.

❿ We had no business _____ with that company.

III. Multiple Choice: *Choose the most appropriate word based on the meaning of the context.*

❶ It is possible to figure _____ how much money we will need for the trip.

(a) in   (b) for   (c) out   (d) at

❷ We are asked to pay _____ the damage of the video player.

(a) for   (b) to   (c) of   (d) by

❸ Bob said he could not think _____ any good hotel in New York.

(a) of   (b) over   (c) upon   (d) out

❹ The students were asked to put _____ tents before 5 o'clock.

(a) out   (b) in   (c) upon   (d) up

❺ Orlando is famous _____ the Disneyland.

(a) as   (b) for   (c) with   (d) about

IV. Cloze Test: *Fill in the blanks with the most appropriate words based on the meaning of the context.*

One of the most famous statues in the world stands on an _____ in New York Harbor. The Statue of Liberty is a woman who holds a _____ up high. Visitors can go inside the _____. The statue is so large _____ as many as twelve people can stand inside the torch. Many more people can stand in _____ parts of the statue.

V. Translation: *Translate the following Chinese sentences into English.*

❶ 自由女神像是法國人送給美國的一份禮物。

_____

❷ 幾年來，法國和美國維持著一個特別的關係。

_____

❸ 法國人想要做些特別的事來慶祝美國的百年建國紀念日。

_____

❹ 美國人為雕像設計及建造了基座以便使雕像能站立起來。

_____

❺ 自由女神象徵著歡迎到美國追尋自由的人。

_____

VI. Discussion Topics: *Discuss the following topics on "sight" in oral or written reports.*

❶ What are the other famous sights in U.S.A. besides *the Statue of Liberty* and *Yellowstone National Park*?

❷ Is there any famous statue in Taiwan? If yes, please describe it.

❸ Imagining you are a guide for foreign tourists, choose a famous sightseeing place in Taiwan and make a brief introduction of it.

Outside Reading

Yellowstone National Park

What do you see in the picture?
Do you know a place like this?

A national park is a large piece of land. In the park animals are free to come and go. Trees and plants grow everywhere. People go to a national park to enjoy nature. Many people stay in campgrounds in national parks. They sleep in tents and cook their food over campfires. They also walk on trails or paths in the parks. On a gate at the entrance of Yellowstone, a sign says, "For the Benefit and Enjoyment of the People."

Old Faithful

Yellowstone is the world's oldest national park. It became a national park in 1872. It is also the world's largest park. It covers parts of the states of Wyoming, Montana, and Idaho. Yellowstone is two-and-a-half times the size of the smallest state, Rhode Island.

Yellowstone is famous for its geysers. These holes in the ground shoot hot water into the air. There are about seventy geysers in the park. The most famous is Old Faithful. About every hour Old Faithful shoots hot water hundreds of feet into the air.

Two-and-a-half million people visit this beautiful park each year. Park rangers give information to visitors. They also take care of the park. They tell visitors not to pick the flowers. They also tell them not to feed or hunt the animals.

Reading Comprehension

1. Yellowstone became a national park in the _____ century.

   (a) eighteenth   (b) nineteenth   (c) twentieth

2. Yellowstone is the world's _____ national park.

   (a) largest   (b) oldest   (c) Both of the above

3. How many states does Yellowstone cover?

   (a) Two.   (b) Three.   (c) Four.

4. According to the author, Yellowstone is famous for its _____.

   (a) animals   (b) plants   (c) geysers

5. Visitors are allowed to _____ in Yellowstone.

   (a) feed the animals   (b) pick the flowers   (c) walk on trails

English Learning Strategy

If I can't think of an English word, I use a word or phrase that means the same thing. （如果想不出一個英文字，我會使用與其意義相同的單字或片語。）

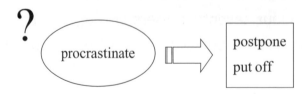

Unit 2

Job Interview

Years ago when you were *looking for* a job, you would present[1] yourself at an interview[2] with a resume[3] *in hand* and be hired because you were well groomed,[4] semiqualified, and somewhat

5 experienced. Things have changed in recent years, though. A large number of very qualified people *are likely to apply for* a desirable[5] position, and in this competitive[6] situation, the impression one makes during an interview can be

10 crucial.[7] Many books and magazine articles are now available to help people compete in this job market and sell themselves to companies, following many of the same techniques[8] used by advertising agencies to market and sell products.

15 Printing companies *boast about* their ability to edit, format, and print quality resumes that will convince employers of their need for you even before you are interviewed. Books on how to dress for success give detailed[9] advice.

20 Other books give advice on how to *prepare* mentally *for* an interview, suggesting that you hire yourself an employer[10] by taking the initiative[11] in

present [prɪˈzɛnt]

interview [ˈɪntɚˌvju]

resume [ˌrɛzʊˈme]

groom [grum]

desirable [dɪˈzaɪrəbl̩]

competitive

  [kəmˈpɛtətɪv]

crucial [ˈkruʃəl]

technique [tɛkˈnik]

detailed [dɪˈteld]

employer [ɪmˈplɔɪɚ]

initiative [ɪˈnɪʃɪˌetɪv]

demonstrate

['dɛmən,stret]

qualification

[,kwɑləfə'keʃən]

persuade [pə'swed]

key [ki]

your meeting with the interviewer. Showing that you have done research about the company, demonstrating[12] that your qualifications[13] are   25 appropriate for the position, and persuading[14] an employer that you are the right person for the job are keys[15] to a successful interview. Even if you are not hired, you will have gained valuable knowledge that will *come in handy* at your next   30 interview.

    Job interviews have become an increasingly important part of the U.S. employment scene, not only *because of* the competition for positions but also because of the growing trend for Americans   35 to have several different jobs during the course of their working years. The rapid rate of technologi-

advance [əd'væns]

likelihood ['laɪklɪ,hʊd]

cal advance[16] and the expanding and changing economy increase the likelihood[17] that a person will have *more than* one or two employers in a   40

phenomenon

[fə'nɑmə,nɑn]

prospective

[prə'spɛktɪv]

lifetime. This phenomenon[18] has created the need for many Americans to learn how to sell themselves to prospective[19] employers.

A. Vocabulary

1. **present** [prɪˈzɛnt] *vt.* to introduce, offer, or exhibit for attention or consideration 呈現;提出

   An opportunity may *present* itself anytime.

2. **interview** [ˈɪntəˌvju] *n.* [C] an oral examination of an applicant 面談

   My job *interview* is on Thursday.

3. **resume** [ˌrɛzuˈme] *n.* [C] a brief account of your personal details, your education, and the jobs you have had 履歷表

   A *resume* is often required when you are applying for a job.

4. **groom** [grum] *vt.* to prepare or train for a particular purpose or job 培植;訓練

   He *groomed* his son for political office.

5. **desirable** [dɪˈzaɪrəbl̩] *adj.* worth having or doing 值得要的;合意的

   Taipei is a *desirable* city for large department stores.

6. **competitive** [kəmˈpɛtətɪv] *adj.* competing with each other 競爭的

   National universities are *competitive* for good students.

7. **crucial** [ˈkruʃəl] *adj.* decisive; critical; very important 決定性的;關係重大的

   Salt is a *crucial* ingredient in cooking.

8. **technique** [tɛkˈnik] *n.* [C] a mechanical skill 技巧;手法

   In order to obtain professional *techniques* about marketing, I observe the marketing section for a week.

9. **detailed** [dɪˈteld] *adj.* containing many details 詳細的

   Tom asked me for *detailed* information about the senior project.

10. **employer** [ɪmˈplɔɪə] *n.* [C] the person or organization you work for 雇主;老板

    Lucy has been sent to America for advanced study by her *employer*.

11. **initiative** [ɪˈnɪʃɪətɪv] *n.* [U] the power or right to begin 主動;率先

He usually took the *initiative* in making friends.

12. **demonstrate** [ˈdɛmənˌstret] *vt.* to show by actions　說明；示範

　　He *demonstrated* how to use the instrument.

13. **qualification** [ˌkwɑləfəˈkeʃən] *n.* [C] an ability, quality, or record of experience fitting a person for a position or purpose　資格

　　These are the *qualifications* for working in this company.

14. **persuade** [pɚˈswed] *vt.* to cause to believe; convince　說服

　　John tried to *persuade* me to believe him.

15. **key** [ki] *n.* [C] means of advance, access, etc.　要訣

　　The *key* to win the first prize is nothing but studying hard.

16. **advance** [ədˈvæns] *n.* [C][U] progress; forward movement　增進；進步

　　I stayed in school after class because I want to make some *advances* in my studies.

17. **likelihood** [ˈlaɪklɪˌhʊd] *n.* [U] possibility　可能性

　　There is no *likelihood* of her gaining my trust.

18. **phenomenon** [fəˈnɑməˌnɑn] *n.* [C] a fact or occurrence that appears or is perceived　現象

　　A rainbow is a natural *phenomenon*.

19. **prospective** [prəˈspɛktɪv] *adj.* likely to be; expected　預期中的；有希望的

　　Jane tells her sister Tom is her *prospective* son-in-law.

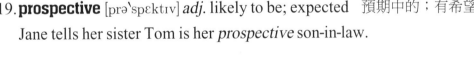

 **. Idioms & Phrases**

1. **look for**　to try to find something　尋求

　　Sam is *looking for* a job to bring up his children.

2. **in hand**　in one's possession; under control　拿在手上地；在控制下

　　I have no cash *in hand* now. Can I pay by credit card?

3. **be likely to** to be probable; to be expected reasonably 有可能…的；可能會…的

It *is likely to* be cold in October.

4. **apply for** to request formally 請求；申請

I usually *apply for* a scholarship to pay my tuition.

5. **boast about** to declare one's virtues, wealth, etc. with excessive pride 自吹自擂

Joe used to *boast about* his rich uncle in California.

6. **prepare for...** to make or get ready 準備

Kara is busy preparing for the lunch.

7. **come in handy** to be useful in a particular situation 可能有用；派上用場

This will *come in handy* to us some day.

8. **because of** on account of; by reason of 因為；由於

Because of the rain, I am not allowed to go out.

9. **more than** greater than 多過

It takes me *more than* one hour to figure out how to solve this problem.

C. Word Forms

1. v. + -ed → adj.

groom（訓練） → groomed（訓練有素的）

experience（經驗）→ experienced（有經驗的）

qualify（使合格） → qualified（合格的）

A cup of coffee will **_refresh_** you.

You will feel **_refreshed_** with a cup of coffee after 5-hour hard working.

2. $\begin{matrix} \textbf{adj.} \\ \textbf{n.} \end{matrix} \}$ **+ -hood → n.**（表示狀況、關係）

likely（有可能的）→ likelihood（可能性）

child（小孩） → childhood（孩童時期）

 We have several nice **_neighbors_**.

We make many good friends in our **_neighborhood_**.

 牛刀小試

1. Jean was so _____ (frighten) that her friends walked home with her.

2. The class is quite _____ (interest) in going to the Natural History Museum.

3. Jackson earns his _____ (lively) by writing novels.

D. Sentence Patterns

1. S. + be likely to + 原形 V.（可能）

 A large number of very qualified people **_are likely to apply_** for a desirable

position.

(1) Tom *is likely to pass* the test.

(2) It *is likely to rain* this afternoon.

2. V-ing + N.P. + V.P.

（動名詞兼具名詞和動詞的性質，在此作主詞用）

 Showing that you have done research about the company, **demonstrating** that your qualifications are appropriate for the position, and **persuading** an employer that you are the right person for the job are keys to a successful interview.

(1) **Learning** English is easy.

(2) **Being** on time makes a good impression on interviewers.

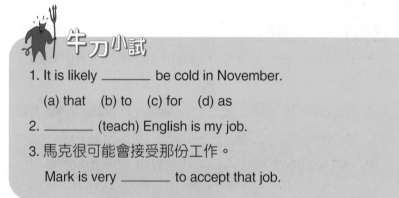

牛刀小試

1. It is likely _____ be cold in November.

(a) that   (b) to   (c) for   (d) as

2. _____ (teach) English is my job.

3. 馬克很可能會接受那份工作。

Mark is very _____ to accept that job.

E . Exercise

I. True/False: *Decide true (T) or false (F) of the following statements based on the text.*

❶ Nowadays you can present yourself at an interview with a resume in hand and be hired.

❷ According to printing companies, quality resumes will convince employers of their need for you even before you are interviewed.

❸ You can prepare mentally for an interview by taking the initiative in your meeting with the interviewer.

❹ Demonstrating that you have done research about the company is one of the keys to a successful interview.

❺ Job interviews have become less important in the U.S. employment scene.

II. Vocabulary Review: *Complete the sentences with the following words of appropriate forms.*

desirable	demonstrate	rapid	technique	phenomenon
available	valuable	competitive	detailed	appropriate

❶ The teacher took _____ action after the accident occurred.

❷ He _____ how the computer worked.

❸ The French government is worried about the _____ decline in the birth rate.

❹ Three small boats are _____ for hire.

❺ Her letter contains a _____ account of the decisions.

❻ There are many scientific explanations of natural _____ in this magazine.

❼ Japan is a highly _____ market compared with Korea.

❽ Prolonged negotiation was not _____ in this meeting.

❾ He went off to the United States to improve his _____.

❿ If you decide to do it by your own ways, here are a few _____ tips that will help you.

III. Multiple Choice: *Choose the most appropriate word based on the meaning of the context.*

❶ More than ten people are applying _____ that job.

   (a) on   (b) for   (c) at   (d) about

❷ We lost much money because _____ the delay of the shipment.

   (a) of   (b) that   (c) for   (d) to

❸ The secretary is looking _____ the keys in her office.

   (a) for   (b) at   (c) by   (d) on

❹ I have sufficient information _____ hand to show you that he is guilty.

    (a) on   (b) of   (c) in   (d) by

❺ Mary is very likely _____ fail the course because she did not spend much studying.

    (a) at   (b) in   (c) to   (d) about

IV. Cloze Test: *Fill in the blanks with the most appropriate words based on the meaning of the context.*

A large number of very qualified people are likely to _____ for a desirable position, and _____ this competitive situation, the impression one _____ during an interview can be crucial. Many books and magazine articles are now available to _____ people compete in this _____ market and sell themselves to companies.

V. Translation: *Translate the following Chinese sentences into English.*

❶ 有關如何穿著以求得成功的書,會提供詳細的忠告。

_____

❷ 說服面試者,讓他覺得你是那個職位最合適的人選,是贏得成功面試的關鍵。

_____

❸ 即使你未被錄用,你將會得到很有價值的知識。

_____

❹ 科技進步的快速,增加了在一生中會有兩個以上雇主的可能性。

_____

❺ 許多美國人必須學著如何將自己推銷給未來的雇主。

_____

VI. Discussion Topics: *Discuss the following topics on "job" in oral or written reports.*

❶ What are your ideas for how to write an effective resume?

❷ What is your ideal job after graduating from school?

❸ Please describe your career plan in the next 10 years.

Outside Reading

Quiz: What Kind of Job Is Best for You?

This quiz is designed to give you an overall view of your career aptitudes and interests. Please answer the following questions YES or NO. There are no right or wrong answers.

1. Do you enjoy games that require concentration, such as chess or bridge?
2. If you had to take a course in school, would you select astronomy, biology, or math rather than history, philosophy, or art appreciation?
3. Do you usually remember specific facts you have read or heard?
4. If you had your choice, would you rather do a few things very well than many things fairly well?
5. Do you keep records, such as budgets, a telephone book of personal and business numbers, and lists of things to do?
6. Do you keep up with new vocabulary in the fields of science, technology, and medicine?
7. As a child, did you enjoy taking things apart to see what made them work?
8. Were mathematics and sciences easy for you in school?
9. If you were given a paid month's vacation to France, would you spend the time exploring Paris or some other place in depth rather than seeing all you could of the entire country?
10. Do you usually prefer novels to factual material, such as biographies, business publications, or scientific books and articles?
11. Do you usually prefer to spend your spare time with people rather than reading, or pursuing a hobby you do by yourself?
12. Do you dislike eating alone?
13. Do you enjoy new people, places, and things?
14. Do you select clothing that has flair and commands attention?

15. Can you do several things well at the same time?

16. Do you usually feel at ease and sincerely interested when you are with people who are much older or younger than you?

17. Do you feel you make lasting friendships easily?

18. Do you enjoy learning new facts and skills even though you cannot necessarily use them at the time?

HOW TO ANALYZE YOUR SCORE:

1. If you have many more YES answers to the first nine questions than the last nine, you are probably someone who enjoys jobs which require patience and attention to detail (scientist, laboratory researcher, accountant, artist).

2. If you have many more YES answers to the last nine questions than the first nine, your greatest strength is in working with people (politician, lawyer, actor, waitress, athlete).

3. If your YES answers are fairly evenly divided between the first nine and the last nine questions, you will probably be best in jobs where you have to work with people and need a good background in your field (teacher, repairperson, banker, librarian, doctor, nurse).

Reading Comprehension

Match the following words or phrases with an appropriate meaning based on the context.

1. quiz	a. continue to learn about
2. at ease	b. short test
3. spare time	c. a lot of experience
4. dislike	d. ability
5. a good background	e. is supposed to
6. in depth	f. comfortable
7. keep up with	g. don't enjoy
8. field	h. subject

9. aptitude
10. is designed to

i. free time
j. as completely as possible

English Learning Strategy

I notice my English mistakes and use that information to help me do better. （我會注意自己所犯的英文錯誤，並且將其作為改進英文的參考。）

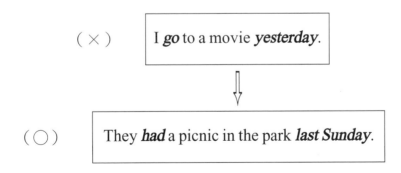

（×）　I *go* to a movie *yesterday*.

（○）　They *had* a picnic in the park *last Sunday*.

Unit  3

Eskimo Art

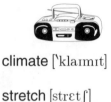

A climate[1] of ice and snow stretches[2] across northern Siberia, Alaska, Canada, and Greenland for most of the year. Nothing grows. It is always cold. But the Eskimos *are able to* live there. They have lived in North America for *at least* 28,000 years. Eskimos call themselves Inuit, which means "people." For *thousands of* years the Inuit thought they were the only people in the world because they never saw other people.

Life in this part of the world is probably the most difficult anywhere.[3] People have only necessary things. But they have developed[4] beautiful art because for them art is very important — it is essential.[5]

The Eskimo artist takes a piece of ivory[6] from a sea animal and holds it in his hands. Slowly he turns it, feels it, and *looks at* it. Then he begins carving[7] the piece of ivory with a knife. As he begins cutting and shaping, he starts to dream. He knows there is a hidden form of an animal in the ivory. As the artist dreams and carves, the animal slowly appears. It might be a seal or a whale. It

climate ['klaɪmɪt]
stretch [strɛtʃ]

anywhere ['ɛnɪˌhwɛr]
develop [dɪ'vɛləp]

essential [ə'senʃəl]
ivory ['aɪvrɪ]

carve [kɑrv]

28

nature [ˈnetʃɚ]

closeness [ˈklosnɪs]

still [stɪl]

exactly [ɪgˈzæktlɪ]

guess [gɛs]

live [laɪv]

handle [ˈhændl̩]

might be a fish or a bird. Eskimos understand animal forms because they live a life *close to nature.*[8] They feel a closeness[9] to the land and to the people and animals that live there. Eskimos know how animals move and how they look when they stand still.[10] The Eskimo artist is able to make an ivory or bone animal that catches the feeling of a living animal exactly.[11]

Why do Eskimos make small animals from ivory? Do these animals have a special meaning in Eskimo society? Social scientists cannot answer these questions. The Eskimos do not tell them, so they can only guess.[12]

A small ivory animal is not just a copy of a live[13] one. It has something of the animal itself in it. Making the animal is more important to the Eskimo artist than owning or keeping it when it is finished. When an artist carves an ivory animal, he or she understands better how it feels to be an animal.

It is important to the Eskimos to feel and handle[14] the small animal carvings. Handling

29

45 makes them smooth, and smoothness[15] improves[16]
the carvings. They become even more beautiful.
Many of the ivory animals do not have perfect
shapes and will not *stand up*. They *fall over* and
roll[17] around. This is not important. People
50 should hold and feel the carvings, not just look at
them.

Small Eskimo carvings of animals, birds, and
people are very popular among people who visit
northern Canada and Alaska. People who cannot
55 visit the area where Eskimos live can see their art
in museums.[18] Most of us never see whales or
seals, but when we see the beautiful form and
color of an ivory or bone animal, we know how
beautiful the real animals are.

smoothness

[ˈsmuðnəs]

improve [ɪmˈpruv]

roll [rol]

museum [mjuˈziəm]

. Vocabulary

1. **climate** [ˈklaɪmɪt] *n.* [C] the weather conditions of an area 氣候
   The *climate* of Australia is milder than that of Britain.

2. **stretch** [strɛtʃ] *vt.* to cover or exist in the whole of an area 延伸；延續
   Desert land *stretches* eastward across Arabia into Central Asia.

3. **anywhere** [ˈɛnɪˌhwɛr] *adv.* in or to any place 任何地方
   I didn't go *anywhere* last night.

4. **develop** [dɪˈvɛləp] *vt.* to make or become bigger 發展；開發
   Don't forget to protect the environment while we are *developing* the natural resources.

5. **essential** [əˈsenʃəl] *adj.* necessary; indispensable 不可或缺的
   Studying hard is the *essential* key to success.

6. **ivory** [ˈaɪvrɪ] *n.* [U] hard substance of the tusks of an elephant 象牙
   It is illegal to import *ivory*.

7. **carve** [kɑrv] *vt.* to produce or shape by cutting 雕刻
   John *carved* his name on the tree.

8. **nature** [ˈnetʃɚ] *n.* [U] the whole universe and every created thing 自然
   The Smith family enjoy the beauties of *nature* by camping on the mountain.

9. **closeness** [ˈklosnɪs] *n.* [C] a friendly feeling to someone or something 親密；接近
   Tina feels a *closeness* to her classmates.

10. **still** [stɪl] *adj.* without moving 不動的
    She has been standing *still* over there for two hours.

11. **exactly** [ɪgˈzæktlɪ] *adv.* precisely 精確地
    Please repeat *exactly* what she told you.

12. **guess** [gɛs] *vi.* to form a hypothesis or opinion about　猜測

   You did not see exactly what happened here so you are just *guessing* now.

13. **live** [laɪv] *adj.* being alive　活的

   Now people can only see fossils of a dinosaur instead of a *live* one.

14. **handle** [ˈhændl̩] *vt.* to operate or manage　處理

   Mom asked me to *handle* this box carefully.

15. **smoothness** [ˈsmuðnəs] *n.* [U] smoothing touch　平滑

   I am impressed by the *smoothness* of the floor in that new-built house.

16. **improve** [ɪmˈpruv] *vt.* to make or become better　改善；
   增進

   Many people take vitamins to *improve* their health.

17. **roll** [rol] *vi.* to move or go in some direction　滾動

   That basketball *rolled* over and over.

18. **museum** [mjuˈziəm] *n.* [C] a building used for storing and
   exhibiting objects of historical, scientific, or cultural interest　博物館

   When I traveled to New York, I visited many *museums*.

B. Idioms & Phrases

1. **be able to**　to have the capacity or power to do something　能夠

   The chairman of the company says he *is able to* keep the price competitive.

2. **at least**　not less than　至少；最少

   About two-thirds of adults consult their doctor *at least*
   once a year.

3. **thousands of**　very many of some things or people　數以
   千計的

   Thousands of refugees from Vietnam were permitted to go to the U.S.A.

4. **look at**　to turn one's eyes in some direction　注視

She *looked at* her parents with a confident smile.

5. **close to** situated at a short distance or interval 接近的

That bookstore is *close to* our university.

6. **stand up** to maintain an upright position 豎立

Wendy is trying to make that big statue *stand up*.

7. **fall over** to lie on the ground or on the surface supporting them 倒下

If he drinks more than two glasses of wine, he *falls over*.

C. Word Forms

1. | **n. + -ern → adj.** |

north（北方）→ northern（北方的）

east（東方） → eastern（東方的）

 My uncle lives in the ***west*** of the USA.

There are many Chinese living in ***western*** America.

2. $\begin{cases} \textbf{v.} \\ \textbf{n.} \end{cases}$ **+ -ist → n.**

art（藝術） → artist（藝術家）

type（打字）→ typist（打字員）

 Sophia's job is to ***type*** the papers for her boss.

She is a ***typist***.

Eskimo Art

牛刀小試

1. Many people from Central American countries decide to find jobs in the _____ (south) U.S.A.

2. Chinese culture is very different from _____ (west) culture.

3. Betty wishes to become a _____ (violin) in the future.

D. Sentence Patterns

1. S. + be able to + 原形 V.（能夠…）

 It is always cold, but the Eskimos **are able to live** there.

(1) My father **is able to speak** five languages.

(2) I **am not able to lend** you the money you need.

2. S₁ + V. + N.P. + where + S₂ + V.P.

 People who cannot visit **the area where** Eskimos live can see their art in museums.

(1) This is **the place where** I spent my childhood.

(2) I will take you to **a store where** you can buy all that you need.

1. I am not able _____ finish this job in three days.

2. They are able _____ work together very efficiently.

    (a) at (b) in (c) to (d) for

3. 威廉先生住的那一間公寓是很老舊的。

    The apartment _____ Mr. William lives is very old.

E. Exercise

I. True/False: *Decide true (T) or false (F) of the following statements based on the text.*

❶ It is very cold in the winter in northern Alaska, but it is warm in the summer.

❷ The Eskimos never saw other people for thousands of years.

❸ For the Eskimo artist, keeping the ivory animal when it is finished is more important than making it.

❹ Many of the ivory animals do not have perfect shapes.

❺ Eskimos do not like to explain the meanings of their carvings.

II. Vocabulary Review: *Complete the sentences with the following words of appropriate forms.*

knife	smooth	museum	develop	real
guess	exactly	climate	bone	essential

❶ Westerners eat with _____ and fork.

❷ Planning is an _____ part of the project.

❸ My grandmother broke a _____ in her leg.

❹ Can you _____ at the price of this T-shirt?

❺ Joy has _____ a good taste in music.

❻ The baby's skin looks very _____.

❼ Mr. Brown is a _____ gentleman.

❽ When foreigners come to Taiwan, they like to visit the Palace _____ in Taipei.

❾ The _____ of Italy is milder than that of Britain.

❿ Do you know _____ the measurements of the table?

III. Multiple Choice: *Choose the most appropriate word based on the meaning of the context.*

❶ This dress will cost _____ least five thousand dollars.

   (a) in   (b) at   (c) not   (d) about

❷ _____ of books are for sale in that bookstore.

   (a) A thousand   (b) Thousands   (c) Two thousands   (d) Many thousand

❸ Mary sat close _____ her husband.

   (a) with   (b) about   (c) in   (d) to

❹ The old man fell _____ a chair in the dark room.

   (a) over   (b) off   (c) apart   (d) upon

❺ I've spend more than one hour making the Christmas tree stand _____.

   (a) out   (b) in   (c) right   (d) up

IV. Cloze Test: *Fill in the blanks with the most appropriate words based on the meaning of the context.*

The Eskimo artist takes a piece of ivory from a sea animal and holds it in his _____. Slowly he turns it, feels it, and looks _____ it. Then he begins carving the piece of _____ with a knife. As the artist dreams and carves, the _____ slowly appears. It might be a seal or a whale. It might be a fish or a bird. Eskimos understand animal forms because they live a _____ close to nature.

V. Translation: *Translate the following Chinese sentences into English.*

❶ 愛斯基摩人對於那片土地及住在那裡的人及動物，感覺很親近。

_____

❷ 一個小小的動物象牙雕像，不僅僅是一個活動物的複製品。

_____

❸ 對愛斯基摩人來說，感覺及處理動物小雕像是很重要的。

_____

❹ 人們必須要拿著並感覺著雕像，不能只是看著它們而已。

_____

❺ 無法親自參觀愛斯基摩居住地區的人，可以到博物館看他們的藝術品。

_____

VI. Discussion Topics: *Discuss the following topics on "art" in oral or written reports.*

❶ What do you think of Eskimo carvings?

❷ Describe the kind of art you like most.

❸ Will you decorate your body with tattooing? Why or why not?

Outside Reading

Body Painting

In many cultures, people decorate their bodies with pictures and designs. Sometimes, the human body is painted or colored with dye, which can be washed off later. Other forms of body decoration, such as tattoos, are permanent and stay with the wearer for life. Very often, people decorate their bodies for a particular purpose, which is reflected in the types of patterns that they use.

The native people of North America made general use of body painting. When warriors prepared for battle, they would paint themselves with bold designs. They concentrated on their faces which were decorated with red stripes, black masks or white circles around the eyes. These designs made the warrior look fierce and aggressive. Other peoples also used war-paint. When the Romans invaded Britain, they found that the ancient Britons painted themselves with blue paint called woad before going into battle.

Body painting can be used for occasions other than battles. The Aboriginal peoples of Australia often decorate their bodies with bold white markings for a corroboree. A corroboree is a special meeting at which men dance and sing.

The Maoris of New Zealand decorated their bodies with tattooing. This permanent form of body decoration indicated the social status of an individual. The more important a person was, the more tattoos they had. Some chiefs and kings had their faces covered entirely by tattoos.

Reading Comprehension

1. Which form of body decoration stay with the wearer for life?

    (a) Dye.   (b) Painting.   (c) Tattoos.

2. The war-paint of North American natives focused on their _____.

    (a) faces   (b) arms   (c) legs

3. The ancient Britons painted themselves with _____ paint before going into battle.

    (a) red   (b) black   (c) blue

4. Native Australians use body painting for _____.

    (a) battles (b) corroborees   (c) the indication of social status

5. Which people decorate their bodies with tattoos?

    (a) North Americans   (b) Maoris   (c) Romans

English Learning Strategy

I pay attention when someone is speaking English.

（當別人說英語時，我會注意聽。）

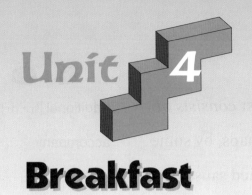

Unit 4
Breakfast

A traditional[1] English breakfast *consists of* bacon and eggs, accompanied,[2] perhaps, by some or all of the following: grilled[3] or fried sausages, kidneys and tomatoes and fried mushrooms. *A*
5 *pair of* kippers[4] is a possible alternative.[5] This main course may be preceded[6] by porridge[7] or some form of cold cereal and accompanied by toast and several cups of tea.

    I do not mean to say that every Englishman
10 eats this much every day, but it is what he has been brought up to think of as breakfast and, time permitting, when he is on holiday, *for instance,* he will *do his best* to get it. It is rather like the Japanese, who, although they may only have *a*
15 *piece of* toast and a cup of tea or coffee most mornings, still think of a Japanese breakfast as being miso soup, fish, nori and a raw egg.

    What we refer to as a continental[8] breakfast is, I suppose, a French breakfast, since, in my
20 experience, the Germans and the Dutch, for example, eat quite a lot more. The French turn pale at the thought of an English breakfast. The

---

traditional [trəˈdɪʃənl̩]

accompany

  [əˈkʌmpənɪ]

grill [grɪl]

kipper [ˈkɪpɚ]

alternative [ɔlˈtɝˑnətɪv]

precede [priˈsid]

porridge [ˈpɔrɪdʒ]

continental

  [ˌkɑntəˈnɛntl̩]

barbaric [bɑrˈbærɪk]

croissant [krəˈsɑnt]

very idea of consuming so much food just after
you have got out of bed strikes them as barbaric.[9]
For them, some coffee and a croissant[10] or a piece   25
of bread with a little jam is the ideal way to start
the day.

delight [dɪˈlaɪt]

    I have been to Paris several times, both as a
student and as a tourist, and I always find the
smell of freshly-ground coffee and freshly-baked   30
bread a delight.[11] Indeed, I love to see people
hurrying through the streets early in the morning,
carrying loaves of French bread which they have
just bought at the baker's and, unable to wait
until they get home, having a taste along the way.   35
I will eat an English breakfast in England and
enjoy it, but in France a continental breakfast is
the only thing. It smells right, tastes right and
feels right.

dormitory

   ['dɔrməˌtorɪ]

refectory [rɪˈfɛktərɪ]

jug [dʒʌg]

    I first went to Paris as a student and stayed in   40
the dormitory[12] of a school. We had our meals in
a long refectory.[13] When we went in to breakfast
each morning, we found several jugs[14] of coffee
and hot milk on each table. At each place there

45　was a basin, like a large cup without a handle,
and a long piece of French bread. Also on the
table were dishes of apricot jam, but no butter.

　　The coffee and milk were poured[15] into the
basin to make café au lait. The bread was split

50　lengthways[16] and jam liberally[17] *spread on*. This
was then eaten as it was, or torn into chunks and
dipped[18] into the coffee before being eaten. It
was very simple fare, but I found it delicious.
Even now, the smell of coffee and freshly-baked

55　bread takes me back to my teens[19] and Paris.

pour [pɔr]

lengthways
　[ˈlɛŋkθˌwez]
liberally [ˈlɪbərəlɪ]
dip [dɪp]

teens [tinz]

A . Vocabulary

1. **traditional** [trəˈdɪʃənl] *adj.* based on tradition   傳統的

   Jason was interested in *traditional* Indian music when he was a college student.

2. **accompany** [əˈkʌmpənɪ] *vt.* to go with; to escort   伴隨

   Please see the booklet *accompanied* for instructions.

3. **grill** [grɪl] *vt.* to cook something by putting it close to very strong direct heat   烤

   Mom *grilled* the burgers for eight minutes each side.

4. **kipper** [ˈkɪpɚ] *n.* [C] a herring or salmon that has been split, salted, and smoked   燻鮭魚

   I just had a *kipper* and some bread for my breakfast.

5. **alternative** [ɔlˈtɝnətɪv] *n.* [C] a choice   替換物

   Jenny had no *alternative* but to report her best friend to the police.

6. **precede** [priˈsid] *vt.* to come or go before in time, order, importance, etc.   於⋯之前

   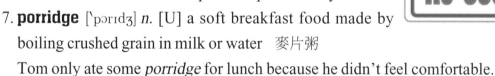

   The numbers on the license plate are *preceded* by a letter.

7. **porridge** [ˈpɔrɪdʒ] *n.* [U] a soft breakfast food made by boiling crushed grain in milk or water   麥片粥

   Tom only ate some *porridge* for lunch because he didn't feel comfortable.

8. **continental** [ˌkɑntəˈnɛntl] *adj.* belonging to or in the European continent   大陸的

   They visited all the major *continental* cities last summer.

9. **barbaric** [bɑrˈbærɪk] *adj.* uncultured; brutal; cruel   未開化的

   It was very *barbaric* of Victor to kill and cook his dog.

10. **croissant** [krəˈsɑnt] *n.* [C] a piece of bread, shaped in a curve and usually eaten for breakfast   牛角麵包

    Coffee and *croissants* are very popular in France.

11. **delight** [dɪˈlaɪt] *n.* [C] something or someone that gives great pleasure   愉快的事

The baby was a great *delight* to its grandparents.

12. **dormitory** [ˈdɔrməˌtorɪ] *n.* [C] a sleeping-room with several beds, especially in a school or institution　宿舍

It is less expensive to stay in the *dormitory* than in an off-campus apartment.

13. **refectory** [rɪˈfɛktərɪ] *n.* [C] a dinning-room, especially in a monastery or college　餐廳

The *refectory* will be full of students when it is time for dinner.

14. **jug** [dʒʌg] *n.* [C] a deep vessel for liquids, with a handle and a lip for pouring 瓶；壺

Mary bought a beautiful *jug* from an old lady yesterday.

15. **pour** [por] *vt.* to make a liquid or a substance such as salt or sand flow out of or into a container　倒

Kevin *poured* some water into a glass.

16. **lengthways** [ˈlɛŋkθˌwez] *adv.* in the direction of the longest side　縱向地

My grandfather asked me to lay the bricks *lengthways*.

17. **liberally** [ˈlɪbərəlɪ] *adv.* abundantly　大量地

Chemical products were used *liberally* over agricultural land.

18. **dip** [dɪp] *vt.* to put something into a liquid and quickly lift it out again　浸泡

The little girl *dipped* her finger in the butter and tasted it.

19. **teens** [tinz] *n.* [C] *pl.* the period of one's life when one is between 13 and 19 years old　十幾歲的少年或少女

Brian and Amy were in their *teens* when they first met.

B. Idioms & Phrases

1. **consist of**　to be composed of　由…組成

Bolognaise sauce *consists of* minced beef, onion, tomatoes, garlic and seasonings.

2. **a pair of** a set of two things which are joined or normally used together 一對

    A pair of teenage boys were smoking cigarettes in the restroom.

3. **for instance** for example 例如

    Wendy is late all the time. *For instance*, she arrived an hour late for an important meeting yesterday.

4. **do one's best** to try as hard as one can to do something 盡某人的全力

    We'll be happy as long as you *do your best*.

5. **a piece of** a part of something that has been separated, broken, or cut from the rest of it 一片；一塊；一張

    The teacher asked each student to take out *a piece of* paper for a quiz.

6. **spread on** to put a soft substance onto a surface in order to cover it 塗

    She *spread* plaster *on* the walls.

. Word Forms

1. $\boxed{\textbf{v.} + \textbf{-ive} \rightarrow \begin{cases}\textbf{adj.}\\ \textbf{n.}\end{cases}}$

  alternate（輪流） → alternative（替換物；二者擇一的）

  appreciate（賞識） → appreciative（有鑑賞力的）

  select（選擇） → selective（選擇的）

 Emily will **attract** a lot of attention in her new dress at the party tomorrow.

  She is quite an **attractive** woman, and the dress is an unusual style.

2. $\boxed{\textbf{v. + -ing} \rightarrow \textbf{n.}}$

follow（跟隨）→ following（下列）
meet（會面）　→ meeting（會議）
spell（拼字）　→ spelling（拼字）

 Most people **greet** each other with a smile.

"Hi", "Hello", and "How are you" are common **greetings** in the United States.

 牛刀小試

1. Please don't tell me the _____ (end) of this mystery story.

2. They are very _____ (cooperate) in completing the project.

3. He has a good _____ (understand) of foreign affairs.

D. Sentence Patterns

1. $\boxed{\text{S. + find + O. + O.C.}}$

 I always **find** the smell of freshly-ground coffee and freshly-baked bread a **delight**.

(1) I **found** it **delicious**.

(2) Tim **found** the book **easy**.

2. **S. + mean + to 原形 V.（有意…）**

 I do not **mean to say** that every Englishman eats this much every day.

   (1) I **mean to study** hard.

   (2) I didn't **mean** Sarah **to read** this letter.

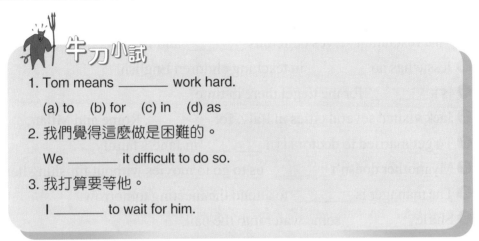

牛刀小試

1. Tom means ＿＿＿ work hard.

   (a) to   (b) for   (c) in   (d) as

2. 我們覺得這麼做是困難的。

   We ＿＿＿ it difficult to do so.

3. 我打算要等他。

   I ＿＿＿ to wait for him.

E. Exercise

I. True/False: *Decide true (T) or false (F) of the following statements based on the text.*

❶ What is referred to as a continental breakfast is an English breakfast.

❷ In the author's experience, the Germans and the Dutch eat a lot more than Frenchmen.

❸ The French do not like the idea of eating so much food after they have got out of bed.

❹ A typical Japanese breakfast includes nori, fish, miso soup and a raw egg.

❺ There were dishes of butter and apricot jam on the table when the author stayed in the dormitory of a school in Paris.

II. Vocabulary Review: *Complete the sentences with the following words of appropriate forms.*

example	possible	grill	consume	pour
tradition	delicious	permit	unable	experience

❶ We had a _____ dinner with Joan last night.

❷ That restaurant serves delicious _____ and fried beef.

❸ Jessie has no _____ in teaching children English.

❹ Is it _____ for me to get there in time?

❺ Jack visited several cities in Italy, for _____, Rome and Milan.

❻ To get married to doctors is a _____ in Jane's family.

❼ My mother doesn't _____ us to go to movies without finishing homework.

❽ The manager is _____ to attend the meeting tomorrow.

❾ Shirley _____ some water into the pail.

❿ Professor William _____ much of his time each day in researching.

III. Multiple Choice: *Choose the most appropriate word based on the meaning of the context.*

❶ Helen always thought _____ her boyfriend when she was studying in the USA.

    (a) for   (b) at   (c) of   (d) to

❷ The United Kingdom consists _____ Great Britain and Northern Ireland.

    (a) of   (b) in   (c) with   (d) for

❸ Little Amy is watching her mother spreading butter _____ bread.

    (a) with   (b) out   (c) on   (d) over

❹ I think a pair _____ gloves is a nice present for my father.

    (a) off   (b) with   (c) up   (d) of

❺ Candy promised me she would do her _____ to prepare this important interview.

    (a) best   (b) most   (c) more   (d) largest

IV. Cloze Test: *Fill in the blanks with the most appropriate words based on the meaning of the context.*

I have _____ to Paris several times, both as a student _____ as a tourist, and I always find the smell of freshly-ground coffee and freshly-baked _____ a delight. Indeed, I love to see people hurrying through the streets early in the morning, carrying loaves of French bread which they have just _____ at the baker's and, unable to wait _____ they get home, having a taste along the way.

V. Translation: *Translate the following Chinese sentences into English.*

❶ 我不意指每個英國人每天都吃這麼多。

_____

❷ 當一想到英式早餐，法國人會臉色發白。

_____

❸ 我第一次是以學生身份到巴黎，並住在學校宿舍。

_____

❹ 當我們每天早上去吃早餐時，會看到每張桌上都有幾瓶咖啡和熱牛奶。

_____

❺ 即使是現在，那咖啡和現烤麵包的香味，仍會讓我想起在巴黎的青少年時期。

_____

VI. Discussion Topics: *Discuss the following topics on "eating" in oral or written reports.*

❶ What do you usually eat for breakfast?

❷ What kind of restaurant do you like to have dinner there?

❸ What is your favorite dish?

Outside Reading

The Right Spot

Suppose you want to open a new restaurant. How would you find the right spot to build the restaurant? How would you make sure that people would go there?

Those questions are important to people who open a new restaurant. They follow certain rules when they build the restaurant. Here are some rules from a company that owns a chain of steak restaurants.

First, choose a town or city that is growing. New people moving in will bring new business to a restaurant.

Build the restaurant on a street that people can get to easily. The street should have plenty of traffic, but the traffic shouldn't go by too fast. About 35 miles per hour is just right. At that speed, drivers will have no trouble turning off the road when they see the restaurant.

Plan a new restaurant near a shopping center, but not in it. A lot of stores together may hide a restaurant.

Finally, open your new restaurant near other eating places. People at other places will notice yours, too. Keep your restaurant away from places just like yours, however. Two steak restaurants side by side will have to share the business.

Reading Comprehension

1. The rules of right spot are provided by a company with a chain of _____ restaurants.

    (a) steak   (b) fast food   (c) sea food

2. According to the given rules, where should the restaurant be built?

    (a) The street has little traffic.

    (b) The traffic does not go by too fast.

    (c) The traffic is about 50 miles per hour.

3. A new restaurant should be opened _____ a shopping center.

    (a) in   (b) near   (c) away from

4. Keep your restaurant away from places _____ yours.

    (a) more expensive than

    (b) cheaper than

    (c) just like

5. Which of the following is NOT included in the rules for opening a new restaurant?

    (a) Choose a town or city that is growing.

    (b) Build the restaurant on a street that people can get to easily.

    (c) Don't open the restaurant near other eating places.

English Learning Strategy

I have clear goals for improving my English skills.

（對於增進我的英文能力，我有明確的目標。）

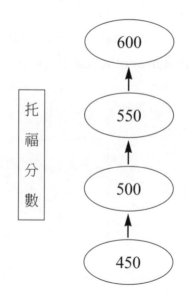

托福分數

600

550

500

450

Unit 5

How Much Exercise Do We Really Need?

How much exercise do you think people need in order to stay healthy?
What kind of exercise is best?

Ellen and David are committed to their
workouts[1] at the health club. They both go every
day *after work* and spend at least one hour doing
vigorous[2] exercise, alternating[3] tough[4] aerobics[5]

5   classes with working out on the machines and
lifting weights. Both are in shape and feel fit.
They *believe in* the motto[6] "No pain, no gain."

Andy and Pam are sitting *in front of* the
television and watching yet another commercial[7]

10 for the local gym.[8] It all seems overwhelming[9] —
going to the gym, working up a sweat, even
finding the time. Neither one is an athlete,[10] nor
do they really care[11] to learn a sport now.

Are you more like Ellen and David or Andy

15 and Pam? Or do you fall somewhere in between?
We all know that exercise is important in keeping
the body healthy and reducing[12] the risks[13] of
disease. It also cuts down on stress and protects
the body's immune system. But for many people,

20 the word *exercise* conjures up hours of boring,
strenuous[14] activity. Recently, however,
scientific studies have found that health benefits

workout [ˈwɝˈkˌaʊt]

vigorous [ˈvɪgərəs]

alternate [ˈɔltɚˌnet]

tough [tʌf]

aerobics [ˌeəˈrobɪks]

motto [ˈmɑto]

commercial

  [kəˈmɝˈʃəl]

gym [dʒɪm]

overwhelming

  [ˌovɚˈhwɛlmɪŋ]

athlete [ˈæθlit]

care [kɛr]

reduce [rɪˈdjus]

risk [rɪsk]

strenuous [ˈstrɛnjuəs]

can be achieved with non-strenuous exercise.

This is very encouraging news for all those

people who thought they *had to* be athletes or 25

work as hard as athletes to make exercise worth

guideline [ˈɡaɪdˌlaɪn]

moderate [ˈmɑdərɪt]

it. The new guidelines[15] say that every adult

should do at least 30 minutes of moderate[16]

activity most days of the week. And these 30

minutes can even be *broken down into* smaller 30

segment [ˈsɛɡmənt]

consistent

   [kənˈsɪstənt]

achieve [əˈtʃiv]

segments[17] during the day. The important thing is

to be consistent[18] and make exercise part of your

daily life.

There are many ways to achieve[19] this

without buying expensive equipment or joining a 35

health club. Walking is one of the best ways to

get exercise. Try to *go for a walk* after lunch or

boost [bust]

metabolism

   [məˈtæblˌɪzəm]

calorie [ˈkæləri]

dinner to boost[20] your metabolism[21] and *work off*

some calories.[22] If possible, walk all or part of

the way to work or school. Use the stairs instead 40

of the elevator whenever you can. Gardening,

raking leaves, and dancing are also good

activities. (However, walking to the coffee or

vending machine doesn't count!) As for sports,

45   even if tennis or golf don't *appeal to* you, hiking and cycling can be relaxing and beneficial[23] too.

    Remember, you can be serious about exercise without taking it too seriously!

beneficial [ˌbɛnəˈfɪʃəl]

A. Vocabulary

1. **workout** ['wɜˈkˌaʊt] *n.* [C] a session of physical exercise or training　運動；體操
   You may give your upper body a *workout* by using handweights.

2. **vigorous** ['vɪgərəs] *adj.* energetic; healthy　強有力的；精力充沛的
   The doctor advises me not to have *vigorous* exercise.

3. **alternate** ['ɔltəˌnet] *vt.* to occur or cause to occur by turns　輪流
   We *alternated* two hours of work and ten minutes of rest.

4. **tough** [tʌf] *adj.* severe; hard　困難的
   The teacher always gives her students *tough* assignments.

5. **aerobics** [ˌeəˈrobɪks] *n.* [U] vigorous exercises designed to increase oxygen intake　有氧運動
   Mary takes *aerobics* every afternoon to keep her body in a good shape.

6. **motto** ['mɑto] *n.* [C] a maxim adopted as a rule of conduct　座右銘
   Peter's *motto* is "Never put off what you can do today until tomorrow."

7. **commercial** [kəˈmɜˈʃəl] *n.* [C] an advertisement on television or radio　廣告
   She'll be back as soon as the *commercials* are over.

8. **gym** [dʒɪm] *n.* [C] a gymnasium, where people go to do physical exercise or get fit　體育館；健身房
   While my father is playing golf, I work out in the *gym*.

9. **overwhelming** [ˌovəˈhwɛlmɪŋ] *adj.* too great to resist or overcome　不可抗拒的
   Jane said she had an *overwhelming* desire to dye her hair red.

10. **athlete** ['æθlit] *n.* [C] a person who engages in athletics, exercise, etc.　運動選手
    He was a great *athlete* and an outstanding coach.

11. **care** [kɛr] *vt., vi.* to feel concern or interest　在意；憂慮

I don't *care* if you go or not.

12. **reduce** [rɪˋdjus] *vt.* to make or become smaller or less　減少；減小

I tried to *reduce* my expenses to save money for a brand-new car.

13. **risk** [rɪsk] *n.* [C] a chance or possibility of danger, loss, injury, etc.　風險

Every one has to run *risks* in their whole life.

14. **strenuous** [ˋstrɛnjʊəs] *adj.* requiring or using great effort　費力的

He made *strenuous* efforts to improve his English.

15. **guideline** [ˋgaɪd,laɪn] *n.* [C] a principle; a directing action　指導方針

I need to find a book that includes *guidelines* on every aspect of running a home.

16. **moderate** [ˋmɑdərɪt] *adj.* avoiding extremes　適度的；有節制的

Being *moderate* in drinking is polite.

17. **segment** [ˋsɛgmənt] *n.* [C] any of the parts into which a thing is or can be divided
部份；片段

I give Tom four *segments* of the orange.

18. **consistent** [kənˋsɪstənt] *adj.* compatible or in harmony　前後一致的；言行一致的

Jim is quite *consistent* in his attitude.

19. **achieve** [əˋtʃiv] *vt.* to reach or attain; accomplish　完成；
達成

Christina has *achieved* her ambition to become a famous
singer.

20. **boost** [bust] *vt.* to promote or encourage; increase　增進；提高

The company is *boosting* their new product.

21. **metabolism** [məˋtæbl̩,ɪzəm] *n.* [U] all the chemical processes in a living organism
for producing energy and growth　新陳代謝

Some people's *metabolism* is more efficient than others.

22. **calorie** [ˋkælərɪ] *n.* [C] a unit of quantity of heat, the amount needed to raise the
temperature of one gram　卡路里

Extra *calories* for a nursing mother are necessary.

23. **beneficial** [,bɛnəˋfɪʃəl] *adj.* advantageous; having benefits　有益處的；有幫助的

Fresh air is *beneficial* to your health.

B. Idioms & Phrases

1. **after work**   in the afternoon or evening after people have finished their work 下班後

   I go to the health club *after work* every day.

2. **believe in**   to have faith or trust in   相信

   Most Americans *believe in* God.

3. **in front of**   ahead of, in advance of   在…之前

   The dog is usually tied up *in front of* the door.

4. **have to**   need, must   必須

   We *have to* study hard to get good grades.

5. **break down into**   to divide into   細分成

   These figures on living expenses can be *broken down into* food, shelter, education, and medical bills.

6. **go for a walk**   to walk; take a walk   去散步

   How about *going for a walk* after dinner?

7. **work off**   to get rid of by work or exercise   漸漸除去；發洩

   I should *work off* excess weight by regular exercise.

8. **appeal to**   to be of interest; attract   引起…的興趣

   Does the movie "Gone with the Wind" *appeal to* you?

C . Word Forms

1. **n. + -ous → adj.**

advantage（優點） → advantageous（有益的）
superstition（迷信）→ superstitious（迷信的）
mystery（神秘） → mysterious（神秘的）
disaster（災難） → disastrous（不幸的）

EX This type of **disaster** usually causes hundreds of deaths and injuries.

The 921 earthquake struck Taiwan and had **disastrous** results.

2. **n. + -ly → adj.**

earth（地球） → earthly（世俗的）
week（星期） → weekly（每星期的）
friend（朋友）→ friendly（友善的）

 Ivy goes to the health club every **week**.

Sam pays a **weekly** visit to his parents.

牛刀小試

1. She walked along the hallway at a _____ (leisure) pace.

2. Elmer could not miss his _____ (day) exercise.

3. The people in that country are very _____ (rebellion) because their government is so unjust.

D. Sentence Patterns

1. | S. + spend + { time / money } + (in) V-ing （花費）

They both go every day after work and **spend** at least one hour **doing** vigorous exercise, alternating tough aerobics classes with working out on the machines and lifting weights.

(1) Professor Wang **spends** thirty minutes in **teaching** grammar.

(2) Are you going to **spend** your whole summer vacations **watching** TV?

Good morning

2. | neither...nor （既非⋯亦非）

Neither one is an athlete, **nor** do they really care to learn a sport now.

(1) John **neither** drinks **nor** gambles.

(2) I love him **neither** for his handsome look **nor** for his wealth.

牛刀小試

1. Tommy spent the whole afternoon _____ the math problem.

   (a) solve (b) solving (c) solved (d) to solve

2. 賈許昨天花了 50 元買那件 T 恤。

   Josh _____ 50 dollars _____ the T-shirt yesterday.

3. Neither Tom _____ Jim likes to drink.

E. Exercise

I. True/False: *Decide true (T) or false (F) of the following statements based on the text.*

❶ David and Ellen believe in the motto "No pain, no gain."

❷ Andy and Pam do not care to learn a sport.

❸ Health benefits can only be achieved with strenuous activity.

❹ The 30 minutes of moderate activity cannot be broken down into smaller segments during the day.

❺ You have to join a health club to make exercise part of your daily life.

II. Vocabulary Review: *Complete the sentences with the following words of appropriate forms.*

athlete	strenuous	commercial	risk	reduce
consistent	segment	achieve	beneficial	moderate

❶ My cousins, Jessica and Monica, like to watch _____ instead of cartoons.

❷ Eugene wants to be an _____ so he takes exercise regularly.

❸ I usually ride my motorcycle at a _____ speed so I have never received a bill.

❹ Belle always eats three _____ of a grapefruit after lunch.

❺ Jack believes that a life without _____ is not interesting at all.

❻ Success is certainly _____ by hard work.

❼ Alice needs to make a _____ effort to pass her English examination.

❽ The government is working hard to _____ the crime rate.

❾ It is definitely _____ for you to practice speaking English every day.

❿ The government should have a _____ policy instead of changing all the time.

III. Multiple Choice: *Choose the most appropriate word based on the meaning of the context.*

❶ Christians all believe _____ God.

   (a) on   (b) for   (c) in   (d) over

❷ Mary usually goes _____ a walk after dinner.

   (a) on   (b) for   (c) in   (d) over

❸ John never works _____ his anger on his wife.

   (a) of   (b) over   (c) through   (d) off

❹ In order to get good grades, Jane has _____ hard.

   (a) to study (b) studying   (c) for studying (d) study

❺ The basketball game does not appeal _____ me at all.

   (a) on   (b) to   (c) in   (d) for

IV. Cloze Test: *Fill in the blanks with the most appropriate words based on the meaning of the context.*

   Walking is one of the best ways to get exercise. Try to go _____ a walk after lunch or dinner to boost your metabolism and _____ off some calories. _____ possible, walk all or part of the way to work or school. Use the stairs instead of the _____ whenever you can. Gardening, _____ leaves, and dancing are also good activities.

V. Translation: *Translate the following Chinese sentences into English.*

❶ 我們都知道運動在保持身體健康及降低疾病風險上很重要。

_____

❷ 運動不但能減輕壓力，還能保護免疫系統。

_____

❸ 近來，科學研究發現健康可由非劇烈性運動獲得。

_____

❹ 重點是持之以恆，把運動視為你日常生活的一部份。

_____

❺ 就算你對網球或高爾夫球沒有興趣，健行或騎單車也能讓人放鬆並且有益。

_____

VI. Discussion Topics: *Discuss the following topics on "exercise" in oral or written reports.*

❶ How often do you get exercise?

❷ What kind of exercise do you like best? Why?

❸ Can you think of any of your family or friends who do not like exercise? If yes, please describe him or her.

Outside Reading

Health Tips for Travelers

Travel is fun and exciting, but not if you get sick. You may think, "Not me. I won't get sick on my vacation!" However, for many people, that is what happens. You do not want to spend your vacation sick in bed, of course. If you have heart trouble, you do not want to make it worse. What can you do to stay in good health? These are the three

things to remember when you travel: relax, sleep, and eat well.

A vacation is supposed to be a time for relaxing, but tourists often forget that. There are so many places to visit: museums, churches, parks, and shops. You want to see as much as possible, of course, and so you spend most of your days on your feet. This is tiring. Your feet may start to hurt. You may get a headache or a backache. If this is the way you feel, you should take a rest. Do not ask your body to do too much. A tired body means a weak body, and a weak body gets sick easily. So sit down for a few hours in a nice spot. In good weather, look for a quiet park bench or an outdoor café. You can learn a lot by watching people while you rest.

Sleep is also important. If you want to stay healthy, you need to get enough sleep. That is not always easy when you are traveling. You may have a noisy hotel room or an uncomfortable bed. If you do, don't be afraid to change rooms or even hotels. If you are young, you may have other reasons for not

sleeping. In many cities the nightlife is exciting. You may want to stay out late at night. Then you should plan to sleep during the day. That extra rest can make a big difference.

Finally, whatever age you are, you must eat well. That means eating the right kinds of foods. Your body needs fresh fruits and vegetables and some meat, milk, or fish. You also need to be careful about eating new foods. Try small amounts first to make sure they are okay for you. And of course, stay away from foods that are very rich.

Remember this: If you want to enjoy your vacation, take care of yourself. Give your body some rest. Get enough sleep and eat good, healthy food.

Reading Comprehension

1. According to the author, which is NOT included in the three things to remember for traveling?

   (a) shopping   (b) sleep   (c) eat well

2. Travelers should take a rest when _____.

   (a) they eat well   (b) their feet start to hurt   (c) they have a noisy hotel

3. Young travelers probably do not get enough sleep because of _____.

   (a) exciting nightlife   (b) different weather   (c) homesickness

4. Eating well means eating the _____ kinds of foods.

   (a) delicious   (b) convenient   (c) right

5. Based on the author's advice, travelers should stay away from _____ foods.

   (a) fresh   (b) rich   (c) new

English Learning Strategy

I encourage myself to speak English even when I am afraid of making a mistake.（即使害怕犯錯，我會鼓勵自己說英文。）

I do not afraid of speak English.

Unit 6

When in Japan

Do you know the customs in Japan for greeting other people? . . . eating a meal in a restaurant? . . . tipping . . . giving gifts? Read the article and find out.

Do you enjoy traveling to other countries? Do you like to see new sights, taste new foods, and understand how foreign cultures *are different from* your own? There is a proverb[1] that goes:

5 When in Rome, do as the Romans do. This means that it is a good idea to try to learn the customs[2] of the place you are visiting, and then behave in a similar fashion.[3]

If you plan to travel to Japan, it might be

10 helpful to know some Japanese customs about public behavior, dining out, tipping,[4] and gifts before you go.

Even though you may *be familiar with* pictures of people in Tokyo crowded into trains

15 during *rush hour*, be aware that people in Japan value[5] their personal space. You might *be used to* touching someone on the arm or giving a pat[6] on the shoulder, but do not do this in Japan. You greet a person by bowing[7] or nodding,[8] or

20 sometimes by shaking hands. If you want to get the attention of a waiter or a salesperson, put your hand out in front of you, palm[9] down, and

proverb ['prɑvɝb]

custom ['kʌstəm]

fashion ['fæʃən]

tip [tɪp]

value ['væljʊ]

pat [pæt]

bow [baʊ]

nod [nɑd]

palm [pɑm]

gesture [ˈdʒɛstʃɚ]

wipe [waɪp]

rude [rud]

treat [trit]

wave it *up and down*. Don't confuse this with the gesture[10] for "No," which is to wave your right hand *back and forth* in front of your face, with your palm facing left.

When dining out, before you start a meal, you will be given a basket with a hot towel in it. Use this towel to wipe[11] your hands and then put it back in the basket. A napkin is not usually used. Be sure to wait until the older people at your table *pick up* their chopsticks before you begin eating.

You will find rice served at every meal. Always alternate a bite of rice with a bite of the side dishes. Don't eat just one dish at a time; this is considered rude.[12] Drink soup directly from the bowl, but don't finish your soup before eating other dishes; it should accompany the entire meal.

When it is time to pay the bill, if the other person has invited you to dinner, let that person pay. If you wish to treat,[13] be the first one to pick up the bill. Don't spend time checking over the

25

30

35

40

45 bill. Honesty is very important and you can

assume[14] that the numbers are correct. And your   assume [əˈsum]

change will not be counted out in front of you; it

will just arrive on a tray. There is no need to

leave a tip, for tipping is almost *unheard of* in

50 Japan.

You will find that gifts are important. You

should bring something when you visit, but it

shouldn't be too expensive or your host[15] will be   host [host]

uncomfortable. Avoid giving four of anything —

55 the word for "four" is similar to the word for

"death." All gifts, even money, should be

wrapped,[16] but your host will probably not open   wrap [ræp]

the gift in front of you, *in order to* show that the

act of giving is more important than the actual

60 gift. Use both hands when you give or receive a

gift.

Remember, people always appreciate[17]   appreciate [əˈpriʃɪˌet]

tourists who respect their customs. Happy

traveling!

74

A. Vocabulary

1. **proverb** [ˈprɑvɝb] *n.* [C] a short saying, held to embody a general truth　諺語

   An old Arab *proverb* says, "The enemy of my enemy is my friend."

2. **custom** [ˈkʌstəm] *n.* [C][U] usual behaviors　習俗；慣例

   The *custom* of lighting the Olympic flame goes back centuries.

3. **fashion** [ˈfæʃən] *n.* [C] the manner of doing something　方式

   There is another drug that works in a similar *fashion*.

4. **tip** [tɪp] *vi.* to make a small present of money for a service given　給小費

   A 10 percent service charge is added in lieu of *tipping*.

5. **value** [ˈvæljʊ] *vt.* to have a high or specified opinion of　重視

   If you *value* your health, you will start being a little kinder to yourself.

6. **pat** [pæt] *n.* [C] a light stroke or tap with the hand in affection　輕拍

   The father gave his son an encouraging *pat* on the shoulder.

7. **bow** [baʊ] *vi.* to incline the head or body in greeting or acknowledgement　鞠躬；彎腰

   She *bowed* slightly before taking her bag.

8. **nod** [nɑd] *vi.* to incline one's head slightly and briefly in assent, greeting, or command　點頭

   Johnson said nothing, but simply *nodded*, as if understanding perfectly.

9. **palm** [pɑm] *n.* [C] the inner surface of the hand between the wrist and fingers　手掌

   He wiped his sweaty *palm* after 2-hour working in the backyard.

10. **gesture** [ˈdʒɛstʃɚ] *n.* [C] a significant movement of a limb or the body　手勢

    Celia made a menacing *gesture* with her fist to express her anger.

11. **wipe** [waɪp] *vt.* to clean or dry (a surface) by rubbing　擦；抹

When she had finished washing, she began to *wipe* the basin clean.

12. **rude** [rud] *adj.* impolite or offensive　無禮的

Unfair bosses and *rude* customers make us unhappy on the job.

13. **treat** [trit] *vi.* to pay another's expenses (as for a meal or drink) especially as a compliment or as an expression of regard or friendship　請客

Amanda said she would *treat* today.

14. **assume** [əˈsum] *vt.* to take to be sure　假定

If the package is wrapped well, we *assume* the contents are also wonderful.

15. **host** [host] *n.* [C] a person who receives or entertains another as a guest　主人

Tommy is always the perfect *host*.

16. **wrap** [ræp] *vt.* to cover (something) in a material folded around　包；裹

Mark had carefully bought and *wrapped* a present for Harry.

17. **appreciate** [əˈpriʃɪˌet] *vt.* to esteem highly; value　激賞

Mary's genius was at last universally *appreciated*.

B. Idioms & Phrases

1. **be different from**　to be unlike, to be of another nature　不同於

This book *is different from* the one I read yesterday.

2. **even though**　despite the fact that　儘管

Even though it was raining outside, Jasmine still decided to go out with Bill.

3. **be familiar with**　to know (a thing) well　熟悉

Having lived in New York for more than 10 years, Jennifer *is* quite *familiar with* the city.

4. **rush hour** times each day when traffic is heaviest
尖峰時段

I had to drive twenty kilometers at *rush hour* every day.

5. **be used to** to be accustomed to 習慣於

I *was used to* getting up early when I was a student at school.

6. **up and down** to and fro 上下地；來回地

The young lady walked *up and down* in the park.

7. **back and forth** repeatedly moving in one direction and then in the opposite direction 來回地

He has paced *back and forth* for two hours.

8. **pick up** to grasp and raise 拿起

After the picnic, the teacher asked students to *pick up* the garbage.

9. **unheard of** unprecedented 未曾有的

The incidence of crime has reached *unheard of* levels.

10. **in order to** with the purpose of; with a view to 為了

He will travel to England *in order to* improve his English.

C. Word Forms

1. **adj. + -y → n.**

honest（誠實的）→ honesty（誠實）
analog（類比的）→ analogy（類似）

 Amy is *modest* about her success.

She speaks with natural *modesty*.

2. **n. = v.**

change（改變）→ change（改變）

need（需要）　→ need（需要）

tip（小費）　　→ tip（給小費）

EX The lawyer will **appeal** to a higher court next week.

He will make a formal **appeal** for a lighter sentence.

牛刀小試

1. Many little kids like _____ (sweet).

2. They are demanding rights of _____ (assemble).

3. Judy believes that _____ (fear) is our worst enemy.

D. Sentence Patterns

1. **S. + be used to + V-ing（習慣於）**

EX You might **be used to touching** someone on the arm or **giving** a pat on the shoulder, but do not do this in Japan.

(1) My mother **is used to getting** up early.

(2) He **is** not **used to being** spoken to in that rude manner.

2. | S. + V.P. + in order to + 原形 V.（為了）|

 All gifts, even money, should be wrapped, but your host will probably not open the gift in front of you, **in order to show** that the act of giving is more important than the actual gift.

(1) Frank gets up early **in order to catch** the train.

(2) Henry is saving money **in order to buy** a basketball.

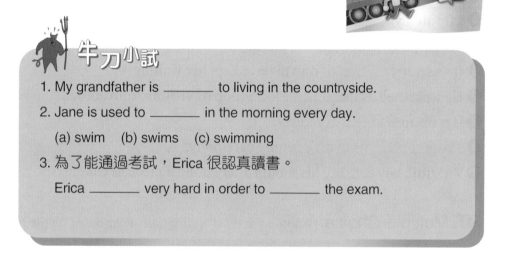

牛刀小試

1. My grandfather is _____ to living in the countryside.

2. Jane is used to _____ in the morning every day.

   (a) swim   (b) swims   (c) swimming

3. 為了能通過考試，Erica 很認真讀書。

   Erica _____ very hard in order to _____ the exam.

 **. Exercise**

I. True/False: *Decide true (T) or false (F) of the following statements based on the text.*

❶ People in Japan do not care about their personal space.

❷ A napkin is not usually used in Japanese restaurants.

❸ Japanese usually drink soup directly from the bowl.

❹ There is no need to leave a tip in Japan.

❺ Japanese usually open the gift in front of their guests.

II. Vocabulary Review: *Complete the sentences by filling in the following words of appropriate forms.*

gesture	respect	invite	avoid	treat
value	host	behave	wipe	rude

❶ He tried to _____ answering my questions.

❷ John's son _____ badly at school.

❸ She used a lot of _____ during her speech.

❹ Lily always _____ your advice highly.

❺ I hope you will _____ his privacy.

❻ It was very _____ of him to have kept her waiting.

❼ He was acted as the _____ to a group of visitors from abroad.

❽ It is his turn to _____ today.

❾ Jessie _____ us to the opening ceremony.

❿ The little boy _____ his mouth after eating a piece of cake.

III. Multiple Choice: *Choose the most appropriate word based on the meaning of the context.*

❶ The goods we received yesterday is different _____ the sample you sent us.

   (a) to   (b) as   (c) from   (d) with

❷ Tom found a wallet and picked it _____.

   (a) out   (b) with   (c) up   (d) at

❸ People on this island are unheard _____ snow.

   (a) to   (b) of   (c) about   (d) with

❹ I was used to _____ up until midnight when I was a student.

   (a) stay   (b) stayed   (c) being staying   (d) staying

❺ Even _____ James is already 70 years old, he goes swimming every morning.

   (a) so   (b) though   (c) for   (d) but

IV. Cloze Test: *Fill in the blanks with the most appropriate words based on the meaning of the context.*

You greet a person by bowing or nodding, or sometimes by _____ hands. If you want to get the _____ of a waiter or a salesperson, put your hand out in front of you, palm down, and wave it up and _____. Don't confuse this _____ the gesture for "No," which is to _____ your right hand back and forth in front of your face.

V. Translation: *Translate the following Chinese sentences into English.*

❶ 有句諺語說：當到羅馬時，就學著羅馬人做（入境隨俗）。

_____

❷ 確定與你同桌的年長者已拿起他們的筷子，你才能開始進食。

_____

❸ 給小費是沒必要的，因為在日本幾乎不曾聽過給小費。

_____

❹ 當你給予或接受禮物時，必須使用雙手。

_____

❺ 人們總是會欣賞尊重他們習俗的旅客。

_____

VI. Discussion Topics: *Discuss the following topics on "travel" in oral or written reports.*

❶ How do Japanese eating customs differ from those in Taiwan?
❷ What advice would you give to a visitor to Taiwan?
❸ Which country would you like most to travel in? Why?

Outside Reading

The Eco-tourist

Tourism around the world is so popular that in certain places it affects and even causes damage to the sights that the tourists have come to see. It is important to think about the economic, cultural, and environmental efforts of being a tourist. So, before you go on vacation, here are some suggestions on how to be an eco-tourist.

1. Use public transport. If everyone uses their cars, pollution and traffic congestion will become an enormous problem.

2. Stay in small hotels and eat local food. It's important that the money you spend on accommodation and food remains within the local area.

3. Travel out of season. It's the best time to avoid crowds, and it's often cheaper too.

4. Think of yourself as a guest, not a tourist. As a tourist, you're simply a source of money.

5. Learn the local language. If you make an effort to speak their language, you'll be able to talk to local people, and they are likely to be even more hospitable.

6. Be careful about taking photos. In some places, people are embarrassed when you take their photo. Find out what the local custom is.

7. Find out about the place you're visiting. It's very impolite to the local people if you're only there because of the weather and don't want to know

anything about where you are.

8. Use less water than at home. In certain places, the authorities supply the big hotels with water.

9. Use local guides. This will create jobs and help the local economy.

10. Adopt the local lifestyle. If you don't appreciate being in a foreign country, why leave home in the first place?

Reading Comprehension

1. To be an eco-tourist, you should stay in _____.

   (a) parks   (b) small hotels   (c) luxurious hotels

2. It is often cheaper to travel _____.

   (a) in season   (b) out of season   (c) on holidays

3. Local people are likely to be even more hospitable when you _____.

   (a) learn the local language

   (b) use public transport

   (c) use less water than at home

4. This will help the local economy when you _____.

   (a) think of yourself as a guest

   (b) are careful about taking photos

   (c) use local guides

5. To avoid the problem of pollution, an eco-tourist should _____.

   (a) eat local food

   (b) use public transport

   (c) find out about the place you're visiting

English Learning Strategy

If I do not understand something in English, I ask the other person to slow down or say it again.（如果英文有聽不懂的地方，我會請求對方放慢速度或再說一遍。）

Can you speak a little more slowly?

OR

I beg your pardon.

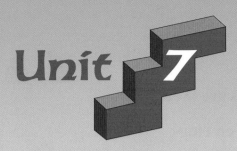

Unit 7

You Love Animals, but Do You Know...?

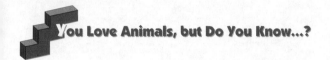

How many different kinds of animals are there?

Fifty? A hundred? A thousand? Ten thousand? A hundred thousand?

No! There are *a lot* more than that. More than
5 one million kinds of animals live on the earth.
When we think of animals, we usually think of
our pets[1], the animals on a farm, and the animals
in a zoo. We forget the creatures[2] that live in the
ocean. We forget insects, worms, and spiders. We
10 even forget birds. They are all animals, too.

To a scientist, an animal is anything that is
alive[3] but is not a plant. The list of animals
includes creatures that are so tiny[4] that we can
see them only under a microscope. And the list
15 includes you, too!

How smart are animals?

No other animals are as smart as people. But
some are very intelligent.[5] Apes,[6] monkeys, and
20 dolphins are the smartest. They can learn to do
many things. Some of them can even solve[7]
problems. For example, a dolphin in a tank was

pet [pɛt]

creature [ˈkritʃɚ]

alive [əˈlaɪv]

tiny [ˈtaɪnɪ]

intelligent
  [ɪnˈtɛlədʒənt]

ape [ep]

solve [sɑlv]

once playing catch with a feather. One time the
feather *stuck to* the side of the tank, high above
the water. The game seemed to be over. But the   25
dolphin figured out how to get the feather back. It

loose [lus]

jumped up and brushed the feather loose[8] with
the side of its head. The dolphin was able to solve
its problem, and the game could *go on*. Most
animals are not this smart. Animals such as   30

clam [klæm]

clams,[9] crabs, insects, and worms are the least
intelligent of all. They can't learn to do very
much. Some can't learn anything.

Do animals talk to each other?   35

Yes, animals do *talk to each other*, but with
"animal talk," not human talk. Animals do not
use words and sentences the way people do. They

movement

[ˈmuvmənt]

express ideas and feelings to each other by using

smell [smɛl]

movements,[10] smells,[11] and sounds. A honey-   40

honeybee [ˈhʌnɪˌbi]

bee[12] does a kind of dance to tell other honeybees

nectar [ˈnɛktɚ]

where to find nectar.[13] A female[14] wolf *gives off*

female [ˈfimel]

a certain smell that tells a male wolf she is ready

mate [met]

to mate.[15] A kitten meows[16] to its mother to let

meow [ˈmɪaʊ]

45 her know it is hungry. A bird sings to warn other
birds to keep away from its nest. These are all
ways that animals talk to each other. Another
animal of the same kind will understand the
feeling or idea being expressed.

50 Some scientists think that dolphins may be
able to talk the way humans do. But *so far* no one
has proved that they can.

You can sometimes hear a lion's roar ten
miles away!

55

How long do animals live?

The longest-living animal is probably the
tortoise.[17] We think it may live more than 150
years. The shortest-living animal is the mayfly.[18]

60 It lives only a few hours. The other animals are in
between. An elephant can live 60 or 70 years.
Your dog or cat will live about 12 or 15 years. A
rat or mouse will live only 2 or 3 years. Some
people say there are parrots that have lived more

65 than 100 years, but no one has proved this.
Parrots can probably live about 50 years. So can

tortoise [ˈtɔrtəs]

mayfly [ˈmeˌflaɪ]

alligator [ˈæləˌgetɚ]

rattlesnake

[ˈrætlˌsnek]

geese, swans, and alligators.[19] Rattlesnakes[20] can live *up to* 18 years, but garter snakes don't usually live more than 5 or 6 years. People live about as long as elephants — around 70 years.

A . Vocabulary

1. **pet** [pɛt] *n.* [C] an animal kept in the home as a companion 寵物
   A rabbit can make a very good *pet*.

2. **creature** [ˈkritʃɚ] *n.* [C] any living being, especially an animal 生物
   The crocodile is a strange-looking *creature*.

3. **alive** [əˈlaɪv] *adj.* living 活著的
   Patsy had been kept *alive* on a life-support machine.

4. **tiny** [ˈtaɪnɪ] *adj.* very small or slight 很小的
   Can you see that young lady holding a *tiny* baby?

5. **intelligent** [ɪnˈtɛlədʒənt] *adj.* having or showing
   intelligence, especially of a high level 智能高的
   Patricia is the most *intelligent* student in her class.

6. **ape** [ep] *n.* [C] a tailless monkey-like primate, e.g. the gorilla, chimpanzee,
   orangutan, or gibbon 無尾猿
   Some people believe that man is descended from the *apes*.

7. **solve** [sɑlv] *vt.* to answer, remove, or effectively deal with (problems) 解決
   Charlie thought money would *solve* all his problems.

8. **loose** [lus] *adj.* not tightly held, fixed, etc. 鬆開的
   The kind little boy set the bird *loose*.

9. **clam** [klæm] *n.* [C] an edible bivalve mollusc 蛤；蚌
   The *clam* is one kind of seafood many people like.

10. **movement** [ˈmuvmənt] *n.* [C] the act of changing position or posture 動作
    Jasmine's *movements* are very elegant.

11. **smell** [smɛl] *n.* [C] the faculty of perceiving odors 嗅覺
    Roy has a good sense of *smell*.

12. **honeybee** ['hʌnɪ,bi] *n.* [C] a bee which makes honey　蜜蜂

That teacher taught his students to observe *honeybees'* habits.

13. **nectar** ['nɛktɚ] *n.* [U] sugary substance produced by plants

and made into honey by bees　花蜜

Bees collect *nectar* from flowers and make it into honey as

their food.

14. **female** ['fimel] *adj.* of the sex that can give birth or produce

eggs　雌性的

Wendy bought a *female* cat from a street vendor last week.

15. **mate** [met] *vi.* to come or bring together for breeding　交配

The lions in the zoo have not *mated* this year.

16. **meow** ['mɪaʊ] *vi.* to make sound (by a cat)（貓）叫

I heard my little kitten *meow* while I came into the house.

17. **tortoise** ['tɔrtəs] *n.* [C] a slow-moving reptile with a horny domed shell　龜

In spite of its slow moving, a *tortoise* may live longer than human beings.

18. **mayfly** ['me,flaɪ] *n.* [C] a kind of insect living briefly in spring　蜉蝣

Mayflies live near water and only live for a very short time as an adult.

19. **alligator** ['ælə,getɚ] *n.* [C] a large reptile of the crocodile family with a head

broader and shorter than a crocodile's　短吻鱷

An adult *alligator* may eat human beings when it is hungry.

20. **rattlesnake** ['rætḷ,snek] *n.* [C] a poisonous American snake with a rattling

structure of horny rings on its tail　響尾蛇

Mr. Smith caught a big *rattlesnake* in his backyard this morning.

B. Idioms & Phrases

1. **a lot**　a large number or amount　許多

Sometimes we have very little snow, but sometimes we have *a lot*.

2. **stick to** to remain fixed on or to 黏住

Mud has *stuck to* my new shoes after a long walking in the woods.

3. **go on** to continue, persevere 繼續

She *went on* with her work after dinner.

4. **talk to** to converse or communicate verbally 交談

Tom *talked to* his classmates when the teacher was distributing the exam papers.

5. **each other** one another 互相

Students are asked to help *each other* in completing this project.

6. **give off** to emit 散發出

This chemical *gives off* an unpleasant smell when it burns.

7. **so far** until now 到目前為止

Which program have you enjoyed most *so far*?

8. **up to** until 直到

Please feel free to call me any time *up to* half past nine at night.

C . Word Forms

1. | **v. + -ure → n.** |

create（創造）　　　　→ creature（生物）

seize（捕捉）　　　　　→ seizure（捕獲）

disclose（暴露；揭發）→ disclosure（發覺；暴露）

 The paper *disclosed* the bribery.

The paper's *disclosure* shocked the public.

2. **v. + -ment → n.**

encourage（激勵） → encouragement（鼓勵）

improve（進步） → improvement（進步）

treat（對待；治療）→ treatment（對待方式；治療法）

 Doctors usually **treat** infections with antibiotics such as penicillin.

A severe infection may require several **treatments** over a long period of time.

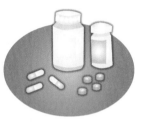

1. Public _____ (expend) should be kept under strict control.

2. The mayor plans to make significant _____ (improve) to all the city parks.

3. Kevin believes that strong parental _____ (encourage) makes children successful.

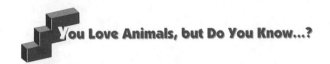

D. Sentence Patterns

1. S. + V. + {
   what
   where
   when
   which
   whom
   how
   } + to + 原形 V.

疑問詞＋不定詞＝名詞片語（通常作為受詞用）

 But the dolphin figured out **how to get** the feather back.

A honeybee does a kind of dance to tell other honeybees **where to find** nectar.

(1) I don't know **how to express** my gratitude to you.

(2) He hasn't decided **where to go** for his summer vacation.

2. So + {
   Be.
   Aux.
   } + S.（也）

 Parrots can probably live about 50 years. **So can** geese, swans, and alligators.

(1) Alice wants to be an English teacher, and **so do** I.

(2) My brother is interested in table tennis, and **so am** I.

牛刀小試

1. 我計畫學習如何操作這機器。

   I plan to learn _____ _____ operate this machine.

2. He asks me when we should leave the school.

   = He asks me _____ _____ _____ the school.

3. John: I went to the party last night.

   Henry: So _____ _____.

E. Exercise

I. True/False: *Decide true (T) or false (F) of the following statements based on the text.*

❶ The list of animals includes plants.

❷ Dolphins can learn to do many things.

❸ A female wolf does a kind of dance to tell a male wolf she is ready to mate.

❹ No one has proved that dolphins can talk the way humans do.

❺ Swans can probably live about 50 years.

II. Vocabulary Review: *Complete the sentences with the following words of appropriate forms.*

female	intelligent	tiny	movement	clam
creature	solve	smell	nectar	mate

❶ Scientists believe that there are _____ in Mars.

❷ Mom always asks me "Why are you afraid of that _____ cockroach"?

❸ _____ students don't get good grades if they don't study.

❹ I always ask my brother to _____ problems for me.

❺ The dancers' _____ were all very elegant.

❻ The dog can find drugs by _____.

❼ _____, crabs and shrimps all have shells.

❽ Do not attack bees' _____ or you will get stings.

❾ Last night I saw two dogs _____ in front of the dormitory.

❿ Is your cat a male or a _____?

III. Multiple Choice: *Choose the most appropriate word based on the meaning of the context.*

❶ I have studied English for more _____ one year.

(a) to   (b) through   (c) than   (d) for

❷ Our discussion should stick _____ one topic.

(a) on   (b) to   (c) for   (d) under

❸ It's not easy to figure _____ how many people are working here.

(a) of   (b) that   (c) for   (d) out

❹ Don't talk _____ each other in class.

(a) to   (b) for   (c) over   (d) between

❺ Some kinds of animals give _____ terrible smell when being attacked.

(a) out   (b) in   (c) off   (d) to

IV. Cloze Test: *Fill in the blanks with the most appropriate words based on the meaning of the context.*

More than one million _____ of animals live on the earth. When we _____ of animals, we usually think of our pets, the animals _____ a farm, and the animals in a zoo. We forget the creatures that _____ in the ocean. We forget insects, worms, and spiders. We even forget birds. They are all _____, too.

V. Translation: *Translate the following Chinese sentences into English.*

❶ 動物包含我們只能用顯微鏡看到的小生物。

_____

❷ 沒有其他的動物跟人一樣聰明。

_____

❸ 動物不像人們一樣使用文字或句子。

_____

❹ 一隻鳥鳴叫以警告其他鳥兒遠離鳥巢。

_____

❺ 據說曾經有鸚鵡活了一百多年。

_____

VI. Discussion Topics: *Discuss the following topics on "animal" in oral or written*
    reports.

❶ Do you like to have pets? Why or why not?

❷ Which animal do you dislike most? Why?

❸ Please describe your opinions of the relationship between humans and animals.

Outside Reading

Animal Communication

Although body language is an important part of animal mating rituals, it is a vital means of communication in many other situations too. Many animals have greeting rituals. When different members of the same species meet in the wild, they may be uncertain whether they are facing an enemy or a friend. So they go through careful greeting rituals to make sure that the other animal does not intend to attack.

Other animals make special signals to warn the members of their species if there is danger nearby. One kind of deer in North America has a white tail. When it is frightened, it runs away with its white tail held upright in the air. The other deer see this warning sign and know to run away too.

Honeybees also use body signals to pass on information. They spend the summer collecting pollen and nectar from flowers to make honey. During the winter, this honey will provide them with food. If a bee finds a large group of flowers, it returns to the hive. There it "dances," flying around in a figure of eight, wriggling and shaking its body as it does so. When the other bees see these movements, they learn where the flowers are and fly out to harvest the pollen.

Like humans, animals also express their moods and feelings through facial expressions. Chimpanzees open their mouths wide and show their teeth when they are frightened or excited. They often pout as a sign of greeting and press their lips together and jut out their jaws when they want to look threatening.

Reading Comprehension

1. Many animals have _____ rituals to make sure whether they are facing an enemy or a friend.

   (a) mating   (b) greeting   (c) funeral

2. The deer in North America uses its white tail as a _____ sign.

   (a) warning   (b) pointing   (c) greeting

3. Honeybees use body signals to pass on information by flying around in a figure of _____.

   (a) three   (b) six   (c) eight

4. Chimpanzees press their lips together when they _____.

   (a) are frightened   (b) greet others   (c) want to look threatening

5. Chimpanzees often _____ as a sign of greeting.

   (a) pout   (b) show their teeth   (c) open their mouths wide

English Learning Strategy

I practice English with other students.

（我會和其他同學練習說英語。）

Unit 8

UFOs: Fact or Fiction?

The existence of UFOs (Unidentified Flying Objects) is a source of controversy[1] that often *divides* people *into* two separate[2] groups: those who believe that UFOs are the spaceships of

5 intelligent beings from other planets, and those who disagree and believe these sightings[3] have some other explanation. Those in the second group say these sightings could be *due to* the effects of a distant[4] planet, a weather disturbance,

10 or airplane lights, for example. Another possible explanation is that the people who report the sightings could be imagining what they saw or *making up* stories to get attention.

Over the years there have been many reports

15 of people seeing mysterious[5] objects in the sky. Sometimes these objects are described as having unusual[6] bright lights. Some people even claim they have been taken *on board* spaceships by alien[7] creatures. Those who insist[8] they have

20 indeed been abducted[9] by aliens have very strange stories to tell. Most of them share the same experiences *such as* being approached[10] by

controversy

['kɑntrə,vɝ·sɪ]

separate ['sɛprɪt]

sighting ['saɪtɪŋ]

distant ['dɪstənt]

mysterious

[mɪs'tɪrɪəs]

unusual [ʌn'juʒʊəl]

alien ['eljən]

insist [ɪn'sɪst]

abduct [æb'dʌkt]

approach [ə'protʃ]

slit [slɪt]

will [wɪl]

occasional [əˈkeʒənḷ]

beam [bim]

awful [ˈɔfḷ]

horrible [ˈhɔrəbḷ]

creatures with large heads on small bodies with slits[11] for eyes. These people say they have been led onto the spaceships against their will[12] and given examinations and tests. After they are returned home, they might experience anxiety with occasional[13] flashbacks and unusual dreams.

One such mystery happened in 1975 in Arizona. Travis Walton, then twenty-two, was traveling in a truck with a group of men when they suddenly spotted a bright object. They stopped, and when Walton got out to get a better look, a beam[14] of light came down and hit him. His friends were so frightened that they *drove off*. They saw the light *take off* into the sky and decided to return with flashlights. They couldn't find any signs of Walton, so they reported him missing.

Five days later, Walton called his sister from a phone booth twelve miles away. He sounded upset and in pain. When he was picked up, he kept talking about awful[15] creatures with horrible[16] eyes that *stared at* him as they led him

25

30

35

40

45   onto a spaceship. At one point he found himself

on an examination table, surrounded[17] by the   surround [sə'raʊnd]

aliens. He was terrified and tried to attack the

creatures, but they left the room. Frightened, he

ran off into another room. He saw other humans

50   there but then *passed out.* When he *woke up,* he

was lying in the road, and saw the UFO take off.

Walton's story has never been proved or

disproved.[18] However, Walton has passed a lie-   disprove [dɪs'pruv]

detector test more than once.

55   Some people who believe they have been

abducted by aliens undergo[19] hypnosis[20] to try to   undergo [ˌʌndəˈgo]

"remember" what really happened. But this is not   hypnosis [hɪpˈnosɪs]

actual proof, for it is possible to "remember"

something that was only a dream. Critics say that

60   many people are influenced by UFO stories they

have read and then use their colorful

imaginations to *come up with* their own stories

and finally convince[21] themselves that these   convince [kənˈvɪns]

events *took place.*

65   Are these people trying to play tricks on us? Are

they confused and possibly showing signs of mental[22]   mental ['mɛntl̩]

    problems? Or are some of them telling the truth?

A. Vocabulary

1. **controversy** [ˈkɑntrəˌvɝsɪ] *n.* [C] [U] (a) prolonged argument or dispute　爭論

   People are very interested in this fierce political *controversy* over human rights abuses.

2. **separate** [ˈsɛprɪt] *adj.* existing apart; different　不同的

   In this gym, men and women have *separate* exercise rooms.

3. **sighting** [ˈsaɪtɪŋ] *n.* [C] a case of seeing something unusual or unexpected 目擊；發現

   The National Weather Service has reported several tornado *sightings* in Illinois.

4. **distant** [ˈdɪstənt] *adj.* far away　遠方的

   No one is worried about the war in that *distant* land.

5. **mysterious** [mɪsˈtɪrɪəs] *adj.* strange and not easily understood　神秘的

   The whole story seems very *mysterious.*

6. **unusual** [ʌnˈjuʒʊəl] *adj.* not usual　不尋常的

   That man likes to plant rare and *unusual* plants in his front yard.

7. **alien** [ˈeljən] *adj.* of beings from other worlds　外星球的

   Scientists are very interested in finding whether *alien* creatures exist or not.

8. **insist** [ɪnˈsɪst] *vt.* to maintain or demand firmly　堅持

   My family *insisted* that I should not give up the study.

9. **abduct** [æbˈdʌkt] *vt.* to carry off or kidnap illegally　綁架

   Jeffery was *abducted* by four gunmen when he was on his way to the airport.

10. **approach** [əˈprotʃ] *vt.* to come near or nearer in space or time 接近

    Children are usually warned not to *approach* any strangers.

11. **slit** [slɪt] *n.* [C] a straight narrow cut or opening　縫隙

Alice watched that young man through a *slit* in the curtains.

12. **will** [wɪl] *n.* [U] the power of mind to decide what to do　意志

My older brother has a strong *will* to win.

13. **occasional** [əˈkeʒənl] *adj.* happening irregularly and infrequently　偶爾的

Mary used to pay *occasional* visits to that old lady.

14. **beam** [bim] *n.* [C] a ray or shaft of light　光束

A *beam* of light from a car swung past my window last night.

15. **awful** [ˈɔfl] *adj.* very bad or unpleasant　可怕的

I met the man yesterday and I thought he was *awful*.

16. **horrible** [ˈhɔrəbl] *adj.* unpleasant　可怕的

The sight of the battlefield was *horrible*.

17. **surround** [səˈraʊnd] *vt.* to be all around on every side;
encircle　包圍

The criminal tried to run away but gave up when he found
himself *surrounded*.

18. **disprove** [dɪsˈpruv] *vt.* to prove (something) to be false　證明⋯為誤

The statistics have *disproved* his hypothesis.

19. **undergo** [ˌʌndəˈgo] *vt.* to suffer; to endure　經歷

New recruits have been *undergoing* training in recent weeks.

20. **hypnosis** [hɪpˈnosɪs] *n.* [U] a sleep-like state in which the subject acts only on
external suggestion　催眠

Brian is now an adult and has re-lived his birth experience under *hypnosis*.

21. **convince** [kənˈvɪns] *vt.* to firmly persuade　說服

The waste disposal industry is finding it difficult to *convince* the public that its
operations are safe.

22. **mental** [ˈmɛntl] *adj.* of, in, or done by the mind　心理的

Scientists find that parents' attitude has a significant influence on children's
mental development.

B. Idioms & Phrases

1. **divide...into...** to separate into parts 將…分類成…；將…分割成…

   The benefits of exercise can be *divided into* three factors.

2. **due to** because of 由於

   The trip was successful *due to* Mr. White's efforts.

3. **make up** to invent in order to deceive people 捏造

   It is very unkind of you to *make up* stories about him.

4. **on board** on or on to a ship, aircraft, oil rig, etc. 登船；登機

   We have to go *on board* before ten o'clock.

5. **such as** for example 像

   The machine cannot work without a fuel *such as* coal or oil.

6. **drive off** to drive a car away（將車）開走

   I *drove off* after waiting in the parking lot for 20 minutes.

7. **take off** (airplanes) to leave the ground and start flying
   起飛；離開地面

   The plane eventually *took off* at 11 o'clock and arrived in
   Tokyo at 13 o'clock.

8. **stare at** to look fixedly 瞪著…看

   Helen continued to *stare at* her father after being blamed by him.

9. **pass out** to become unconscious 失去知覺

   She felt sick and dizzy and then *passed out*.

10. **wake up** to cease to sleep 醒來

    One morning I *woke up* and felt something was wrong.

11. **come up with** to produce 提出

    One of the students has *come up with* solutions for the problem.

12. **take place** to occur 發生

The Presidential Election *took place* on March 18.

C . Word Forms

1. **n. + -ible → adj.**

horror（恐怖）→ horrible（恐怖的）

terror（驚恐）→ terrible（駭人的）

sense（感覺）→ sensible（能感覺到的）

 He has a keen *sense* of hearing.

He was *sensible* of a voice calling him from far.

2. **adj. + -ify → v.**

terrific（可怕的）→ terrify（使恐懼）

simple（簡單的）→ simplify（簡化）

pure（純淨的）→ purify（淨化）

 A storm arose on the ocean and *intensified* in severity. The captain of the ship became worried.

He overcame his *intense* feeling of fear and organized the crew to try to save the ship.

1. The police is investigating the _____ (terror) murder.

2. Mr. Wang did not _____ (specific) exactly what to do, so many people get confused and frustrated.

3. Because the salesperson did not _____ (clear) the directions, Judy couldn't start up her new computer.

D. Sentence Patterns

1. S. + see + O. + 原形 V.

（see, hear, behold, feel, watch, observe, perceive, notice, look at, listen to 等為感官動詞，後面須接原形動詞）

 They *saw* the light *take* off into the sky and decided to return with flashlights. When he woke up, he was lying in the road, and *saw* the UFO *take* off.

(1) I *heard* the people *talk* to each other.

(2) He *felt* the house *shake*.

2. It is + Adj. + to 原形 V.

（it 是形式上的主詞，to 所引導的不定詞片語才是真正的主詞）

 But this is not actual proof, for *it* is possible *to "remember" something that was only a dream*.

(1) *It* is wrong *to cheat in exams*.

(2) **It** is always difficult for Jim **to be on time**.

牛刀小試

1. Nobody perceived Tom _____ the warehouse.

   (a) entered   (b) was entering   (c) enter

2. _____ _____ impossible for me to get up at six.

3. 要精通數種外語是困難的。

   _____ is hard _____ master several _____ languages.

E. Exercise

I. True/False: *Decide true (T) or false (F) of the following statements based on the text.*

❶ Most people believe that UFOs are the spaceships of intelligent beings from other planets.

❷ One possible explanation for UFOs is that the people who report the sightings could be making up stories to get attention.

❸ Some people claim they have been taken on board spaceships by alien creatures.

❹ Walton's story about being abducted by aliens has been disproved.

❺ It is possible that people could remember something that was only a dream.

II. Vocabulary Review: *Complete the sentences by filling in the following words of appropriate forms.*

alien	mental	mysterious	approach	will
separate	hypnosis	abduct	usual	occasional

❶ Most people entered the pyramid died of a _____ illness.

❷ It is _____ for him to enter a room without knocking on the door first.

❸ Everybody begins to ask me about my plan because the summer vacation is

_____.

❹ Although he is an _____ customer, we still have to meet his needs.

❺ She is so sick that she lost her _____ to live.

❻ My parents have been living _____ for years.

❼ John believes that someday the _____ on Mars will start attacking the earth.

❽ Some people think appropriate _____ can cure illness.

❾ A _____ patient is like a bomb in our society.

❿ There were several _____ in this city last month.

III. Multiple Choice: *Choose the most appropriate word based on the meaning of the context.*

❶ More than one thousand people _____ board the Titanic died.

   (a) to   (b) on   (c) under   (d) in

❷ Jenny is quite good at making _____ excuses.

   (a) out   (b) to   (c) up   (d) on

❸ I used to skip classes in order to see the plane take _____ .

   (a) out   (b) up   (c) in   (d) off

❹ All classmates stared _____ me when I was punished for cheating.

   (a) at   (b) on   (c) to   (d) upon

❺ The car accident took _____ while I was thinking about my wife.

   (a) off   (b) place   (c) out   (d) occasion

IV. Cloze Test: *Fill in the blanks with the most appropriate words based on the meaning of the context.*

Over the years there _____ been many reports of people seeing mysterious objects in the sky. Sometimes these _____ are described as having unusual bright lights. Those _____ insist they have indeed been abducted by aliens have

very strange stories to _____. Most of them share the same experiences such as _____ approached by creatures with large heads on small bodies with slits for eyes.

V. Translation: *Translate the following Chinese sentences into English.*

❶ 幽浮的存在一直是個分成兩派的爭議性話題。

_____

❷ 五天後，Walton 遠從十二哩外的電話亭打電話給他姊姊。

_____

❸ 然而，Walton 不只一次通過測謊器。

_____

❹ 很多人受他們所讀過的幽浮故事影響，進而運用自己生動的想像力創造他們自己的故事。

_____

❺ 這些人是在耍我們嗎？

_____

VI. Discussion Topics: *Discuss the following topics on "UFO" in oral or written reports.*

❶ Do you believe in the existence of UFOs? Why or why not?
❷ Please describe the appearance of aliens based on your impression or imagination.
❸ What do you think of those people who claimed to have been abducted by aliens?

Outside Reading

Lost in the Bermuda Triangle

Find Florida on a map. Then locate the islands of Bermuda and Puerto Rico. Draw a line from the base of Florida to Bermuda to Puerto Rico and back to Florida. You will plot a triangle. The part of ocean inside is known as the Bermuda Triangle.

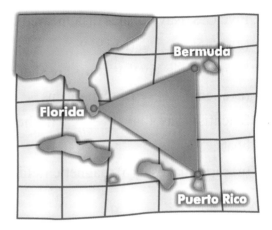

The Bermuda Triangle is a strange area. It frightens many people who fly or sail through it. Several airplanes and boats have disappeared there.

Here are just a few of the mysteries.

In 1945, five U.S. Navy planes flew out from Florida. They all disappeared. A boat was sent out. Its object was to find the planes. No one ever saw the boat or its 13-man crew again.

In 1967, a boat called the *Witchcraft* left Miami. At 9 p.m. the captain said his boat had hit something. It took only 15 minutes for a Coast Guard cutter to get to where the captain said he was. All the cutter found at the scene was empty water. Divers went under the water. They found nothing there either.

What is behind these mysteries? Some people say that creatures from another planet live in the Bermuda Triangle. They shoot down the planes and boats. Scientists don't agree. They say that strong winds and storms in the area bring down the different craft. They also say the water current is very strong there. A boat that sinks can be carried far away before divers go down to look for it.

Reading Comprehension

1. The Bermuda Triangle is located among Bermuda, Puerto Rico, and _____.

    (a) Mexico   (b) Texas   (c) Florida

2. The Bermuda Triangle refers to a strange area of _____.

    (a) desert   (b) ocean   (c) sky

3. Five U.S. Navy planes disappeared in the Bermuda Triangle in _____.

    (a) 1945   (b) 1959   (c) 1967

4. Some people say that crafts are shot down in the Bermuda Triangle by _____.

    (a) aliens   (b) Americans   (c) Russians

5. Scientists say that _____ in the Bermuda Triangle bring down planes and boats.

    (a) earthquakes   (b) magnetic fields   (c) strong winds and storms

English Learning Strategy

I try to learn about the culture of English speakers.

（我會試著去學習美（英）國文化。）

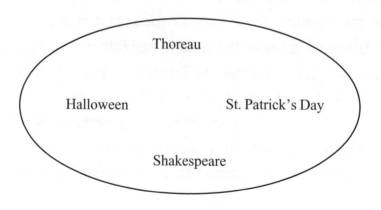

Index I

Vocabulary

Idioms & Phrases

UP-TO-DATE!!

清楚 · 明瞭 · 方便 · 易查

三民 **簡明** 英漢辭典 《全新修訂版》

◎ 內容涵蓋70,074個詞條，從日常生活用語到專業用語，一應俱全。

◎ 大量收錄了符合現代潮流的新辭彙、新語義。

◎ 精準明確的譯義，有助讀者快速理解。

◎ 全書採用K.K.音標，並清楚標示美音／英音差異。

◎ 有＊、＊記號的重要字彙，均有套色印刷設計，方便易查。

◎ 輕巧體貼的口袋型設計，便於外出攜帶。

第一本專為華人青少年編寫
以華人生活為主題的英文課外讀物

黛安的日記 ①

黃啟哲　著／呂亨英　譯

　　如果你認為上英文課已經很苦了，想想看，要是你突然發現要搬到美國，並且必須跟美國小孩一起上學的話，會是什麼情況呢？這事就發生在黛安身上。想知道一個完全不會英文的中國小女孩在美國怎麼生存的嗎？看黛安的日記吧！

你覺得學習英文很難、很痛苦嗎？
那麼，就讓我們幫你把它變有趣吧！

《英文自然學習法一》

《英文自然學習法二》

《英文自然學習法三》

《自然英語會話》

大西泰斗著・Paul C. McVay／著

生活化、實用化的內容
讓您使用英文就像母語一樣自然！